THE DADDY PLAN

KAREN ROSE SMITH

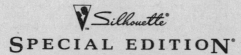

SPECIAL EDITION

Published by Silhouette Books

America's Publisher of Contemporary Romance

SILHOUETTE BOOKS

ISBN-13: 978-0-373-24908-4
ISBN-10:   0-373-24908-X

THE DADDY PLAN

Visit Silhouette Books at www.eHarlequin.com

Printed in U.S.A.

Chapter One

"Will you donate your sperm so I can have a baby?" Corrie Edwards asked her boss.

At his family's cabin in Minnesota's snowy woods, Sam Barclay didn't know whether to laugh out loud or head to the lake for ice-fishing.

Six weeks ago, he'd driven to the cabin to escape the holidays, take a vacation from his veterinary practice, forget his broken engagement and get a perspective on his life.

"You *are* kidding, right?" His veterinary assistant didn't understand how much the question unsettled him. He'd called off his wedding because his fiancée had hidden her abortion from him.

"I'm serious, Sam," Corrie answered with a determined look. "I didn't drive four hours in this weather without a good reason."

She was still dressed in her yellow parka, snowflakes

melting in her curly red-brown hair. He and his partner had hired her three years ago as a veterinary assistant after they'd bought the clinic.

Studying the brightness of her blue eyes, the dance of freckles across her nose, he felt a tightening in his gut he didn't want to recognize. This was Corrie for heck's sake! He was her boss. They talked about animals, the weather and life in Rapid Creek. They'd never had a "personal" conversation.

But you shared, one out-of-this-world, earthshaking kiss, a nudging voice inside his head reminded him.

That had been two years ago...before Alicia.

"Take off your coat and tell me what this is all about. I'll make a pot of coffee."

As Corrie slipped off her parka and hung it over a straight-backed chair, Sam noticed the way her blue sweater fell over her breasts, how the fabric hung free of her very slim waist. Her legs were long in her stretch leggings and high boots.

Desire kicked him and forced him to concentrate on making coffee in the galley kitchen. Still, he was aware of Corrie gravitating toward Patches. His brown-and-black mutt had the distinguishing attributes of a Labrador, but about ten other breeds mixed in, too. Jasper, a small buff-colored cocker spaniel who trailed into the cabin with Corrie, had settled down in Patches's big bed. His dog didn't seem to mind. Patches flopped down in front of Corrie, thrilled to have her scratch his ears.

For some insane reason, Sam suddenly wondered what Corrie's touch might feel like—

He swore.

"Something wrong?" she asked, glancing toward him.

The cabin was too small to hide a sound or much of anything else.

As her eyes roamed over his face, dropped to his flannel shirt and jeans, he had the feeling she was sizing him up…or else his genes?

He felt heat crawl up under his scruffy week-old beard. "Nothing's wrong. The coffee will be ready in a few minutes."

As he lowered himself beside her on the sofa, he felt her tense, saw her shoulders square a bit, her chin go up as if she were ready for a fight or an argument.

Corrie, a fighter?

It was as if her question had unlocked a box that he'd always designated for steady, melt-into-the-background Corrie Edwards and someone else had popped out.

Gently, he asked, "So you want to be a mother?"

When she looked at him, her eyes were shiny with emotion. "I've *always* wanted to be a mother. I've just never met the right man. I don't think I ever will. I'm not getting any younger."

His protest came easily. "You're only thirty-three." A year older than he was.

"Thirty-three might be young as far as the rest of my lifetime goes, but in child-bearing years—" She shook her head. "I have a classmate in Minneapolis who's thirty-eight. She got pregnant and was doing just fine, then all of a sudden she developed preeclampsia. She almost died. I have another friend in St. Paul who's thirty-five. She just had her first baby. Her daughter is six months old, but she never imagined raising her would be so difficult—that she wouldn't have the energy she used to have. She's so exhausted day after day."

"That doesn't mean *you'd* be like that."

"I know. But I *really* want to be a mother, Sam. A mom like my mother was to me. Each year that passes my eggs are getting older and I'm not as fertile. I don't want to end up childless because I didn't do this soon enough."

"And my sperm qualify because…?" He waited, needing to know why she'd come to *him*.

She laid her hand on his arm. "You're…" She paused and flushed a bit. "You're great-looking. You're a good age. And you're wonderful with Kyle. I've seen you with him."

His nephew Kyle, who was five, was one of his favorite people. In fact, he liked kids as much as animals. They didn't have ulterior motives and their reactions were honest.

"I'm flattered, Corrie, really I am. But becoming a father this way—" Her hand on his arm was damn distracting. He had the feeling she didn't even know it was there. After all, they were just boss and employee. They'd always pretended that kiss had never happened.

She removed her hand from his forearm. "You don't have to be a father in the real sense. I mean, this could just be a business arrangement. You donate your sperm and that's that."

He'd donate his sperm and *that* was *that*? "If you got pregnant and I had a child, don't you think I'd want to be in his life?"

"I don't know. Would you?"

He thought about Alicia, what she'd done, the sorrow he'd felt, the absolute sense of betrayal. He couldn't imagine having a child and not wanting to be part of his or her life. "Do you know how sticky this could get?"

"Or *not*." She put the emphasis on the not. "If I became pregnant, if I have a baby, I would want a male role model in his or her life. You could fit in that way. As I said, I've seen you with Kyle. You'd be great. But I also know your brother Nathan said you're researching setting up veterinary clinics in foreign countries. If you decide that's something you want to do, you wouldn't have any strings tying you here."

"A child is one awfully big string."

Corrie studied him. "I thought men just wanted to donate their sperm then shirk responsibility."

"Where did you get your opinion of men?"

Corrie's cheeks reddened. "It doesn't matter where my opinion comes from, does it? I just don't believe becoming a father is on most men's agendas when they have sex. They walk away as soon as something goes wrong…as soon as they see someone else they'd rather be with."

Sam wanted to shout, *That's not true. My mother was the one who walked away.* But he didn't. Corrie's opinion was Corrie's opinion. Something obviously had happened to her to make her believe it. Hadn't he himself concluded in the past few weeks that he was destined to be a bachelor? His father had trusted a woman and she'd walked out on her husband and kids. Sam had taken a chance on love and had been hurt just as badly.

"Let me tell you something, Corrie. If I *were* to father a child, I would *not* shirk my responsibility. That's something you'd have to decide whether you could live with or not."

Her eyes widened. "I never expected you'd want to be…involved."

Because after their kiss in the tavern that New Year's Eve they'd ignored the chemistry, ignored the possibility of connection? Why *had* he ignored it?

The answer came swiftly. He'd sensed Corrie had walls he'd have difficulty breaking down. Besides neither of them had wanted to tamper with a boss-employee relationship that worked. Apparently neither of them had been ready for a relationship much more intimate than that.

He was aware of a pleasant scent that always seemed to surround Corrie, something like peaches and vanilla. It must be a lotion she used or a shampoo. Right now, inhaling it, studying her heart-shaped face, the wild mass of auburn curls, the scent wrapped itself around him.

Needing that cup of coffee, he rose to his feet and went to the kitchen. Her gaze followed him, and he found himself unnerved by her proposition. He should just say no. Why was he even considering it?

Because becoming a dad, even in this way, could give purpose to his life? A purpose it didn't have now?

Jasper suddenly decided he'd had enough of a nap. He stood, shook himself and came trotting over to Sam to look up at him expectantly.

"What can I do for you?" Sam asked, eager to change the subject, at least for a little while until he got his thoughts together.

"Whenever I go to my kitchen, he wants a treat. I have a few in my coat pocket."

Before Corrie could rise from the sofa, Sam said, "I'll get them." He went to her coat and found a bag. He took out a treat. The pup stood up on hind legs and danced around Sam until Sam dropped it into his mouth.

"You haven't told me why you're taking care of Shirley Klinedinst's dog."

The expression on Corrie's face changed and her voice lowered. "Shirley passed on two weeks ago."

"Oh, Corrie, I'm sorry." He knew Corrie and the older woman had gotten close. Shirley's old farmhouse on the outskirts of town had been too much for her to handle and had fallen into disrepair. Shirley had had no relatives in town and Sam knew Corrie had stopped in at least once a week to check on her and help out.

"Her lawyer called me after she was taken to the hospital and said he had instructions to bring Jasper to me if anything happened to her...at least until her estate is settled. Apparently she made some kind of arrangement for Jasper in her will. I said I'd take care of him, of course."

As soon as Jasper finished crunching on his treat, he ran over to Corrie and jumped up onto the sofa beside her. She laughed and hugged him and Sam felt himself touched in some way. Oh, he saw Corrie with animals every day. She handled them confidently and expertly. But seeing her with Jasper now...was different somehow. In his mind, he imagined her growing large with child, cuddling the baby after it was born, chasing after a toddler. The Corrie Edwards he was seeing today was very different from the one he'd summarily dismissed the past few years.

Was the change in *him* today, or was it in her?

Or had the question she'd asked him changed his perception of her? Maybe that question had made him see her as a woman rather than an employee.

"You can't drive back this evening, you know."

Her head came up and her gaze locked to his. "Why not?"

"You're going to be snowed in. The crews won't clear this road until the snowplows take care of the interstate."

"I have four-wheel drive."

"Be realistic, Corrie. It's already getting dark. What if

you get stranded? There's no cell phone reception. You couldn't even call me."

She looked down at the little cocker spaniel, and he knew she was thinking about Jasper, too. She wouldn't do anything to put that animal in harm's way. "I didn't plan on staying. I didn't bring extra clothes—"

"Or a toothbrush?" he teased. "What? You were planning to run in here, drop that question on me, then run out again? Why didn't you just wait until I came back? Nathan and Sara's wedding is next weekend, and I can't miss it."

"I heard about the wedding. But honestly, that's another reason I drove up here today. I thought it might be awkward working together until you gave me an answer. I didn't want you to feel…pressured."

"Once I give you my decision, we'll still be working together."

"I know. But if you don't want to do it, we'll just go on as if I never asked."

In other words, Corrie wanted him to give this plan of hers serious thought without any distractions.

Sam's knee brushed hers as he shifted toward her. "You want me to consider your idea seriously."

Her eyes grew shiny. "This means a lot to me, Sam."

He knew Corrie had lost her mom shortly before taking the job with him and Eric, but he didn't know much else about her background. "Do you have brothers or sisters…family?"

"My dad is in Minneapolis. But we're…not close. I always wanted brothers and sisters. You're lucky to have two brothers." Corrie sounded wistful.

"Nathan and Ben are great when they mind their own business. But every once in a while, they're not busy enough with their own lives and think they have to poke into mine." Sam was the youngest, Nathan the eldest and soon to be a newlywed. These days Nathan's fiancée, Sara, and his son Kyle were his sole focus. Ben was the middle brother, an Assistant District Attorney in Albuquerque, New Mexico, and a cynic about women and life.

"When I was a kid, Ben, Nathan and I were like the Three Musketeers. One for all and all for one. I can't imagine not having that support. Were you lonely?"

"Sometimes," she admitted. "But that's why I took in strays and found them homes."

He'd always known Corrie was a woman who cared deeply. He could tell because of the way she handled animals. Now he saw there was a depth to her he'd never noticed before. Depth and natural beauty.

If they had a baby together…

A baby.

The thought was running around in his head as if it might want to find a permanent place there. Sitting so close to Corrie, he had the sudden desire to stroke her hair behind her ear, to taste her pretty pink lips—

"We should probably take the dogs out before the snow gets any deeper and the temperature drops for the night," he decided gruffly.

As he went to the hook beside the door for his ski jacket to brave the January night, he couldn't help thinking about the fact that Corrie wanted to have *his* baby. The idea definitely fed his ego.

But it also created turmoil.

Because of what Alicia had done?

He had to figure out the answer before he could give Corrie a yes or a no.

* * *

Corrie was ready to jump out of her skin.

Spend the night with Sam Barclay in his cabin? She'd never imagined that in her wildest dreams. Well, maybe she had. Maybe that was the problem.

She felt Sam's gaze on her as she pretended to watch Jasper romp in the snow. After Patches chased him, the smaller dog returned the favor. All the while, she knew Sam was trying to figure out exactly who she was.

She was a woman who'd had a crush on her boss since she'd been hired. She was a woman who didn't really attract men because she didn't want to with good reason. Her father had been unfaithful to her mother. Corrie would *never* forget the day she had walked in on him and witnessed that infidelity firsthand. It had changed her relationship with her parents forever. When she'd fallen in love in college, she'd learned the guy hadn't been in love with her. After they'd made love, he'd moved on to the next challenge, and she'd learned she'd been a dare and a notch on his belt. That experience had set her up to steer clear of any romantic entanglement.

She hadn't wanted to be attracted to Sam Barclay after he and his partner had hired her. But there was something about his grin, something about his gentle eyes, something about the way he talked to animals that had gotten to her. And then there had been that New Year's Eve kiss almost two years ago. But afterward he'd never looked her way again. He'd been too busy making a success of the clinic with Eric. And then, last year, he'd fallen hard for travel agent, Alicia Walker, whom he'd met when he was planning a trip to Africa to a game preserve. He and Alicia had been an item until this past August.

No one seemed to know why the couple had broken up, but Corrie had seen how devastated Sam was. She'd worried about him when he'd left for these woods before Thanksgiving, but she'd also realized *she* had to make something happen in her own life. That had been her New Year's resolution. It had taken her the past two weeks to find the courage to drive up here.

She'd kept asking herself—*What's the worst that can happen?* He could say no.

If he did, she'd go to a fertility clinic in Minneapolis.

But he hadn't said no yet and that gave her hope.

The wind was picking up. Shivering, Corrie headed for the cabin with Jasper following. "See you inside," she said brightly as if spending the night with Sam was no big deal, as if the quiet of the cabin wouldn't have to be filled with conversation, as if she wouldn't be aware of every move he made, every word he uttered, every glance he cast her way.

Sam was her boss. She had to play this right because whether he said yes or no, she didn't want to get fired.

Just as he called to her—"Watch out, that bottom step gets slippery"—she found out for herself. Her boot slipped and she would have ended up as a pile in the snow if Sam hadn't been right there, his arms circling her, his cheek almost brushing hers.

"Are you okay?" His voice was low and husky, his breath warm against her skin. "You didn't turn your ankle did you?"

Because Sam hadn't shaved for a while, the stubble on his jaw was as dark as his brown hair. He was so sexy that even with the temperature dropping, hers was warming up.

After gulping in one very cold breath, she managed to say, "My ankle's fine."

"I'll help you up the steps." He was still looking at her, and she had the weird sensation he was really seeing her for the first time. They'd worked around each other for three years yet this awareness hadn't been there before. Maybe it was all on her part. After all, she'd always hidden her attraction to him, never let it peek out.

His large hand under her elbow, Sam made sure her footing was secure and steered her to the door. As she opened it and stepped inside, he whistled to Patches and the big dog came running.

Both dogs shook snow from their coats and sent flakes flying.

"Do you have a towel I can use on Jasper?" Corrie asked Sam. "I don't want his fur to get all matted."

"Sure, I'll look for something for you to wear, too."

"For me to wear?"

"You don't want to sleep in your clothes do you?"

She hadn't really thought about it. "I can."

"No need," he said with a shrug. "I have a flannel shirt that will probably fall to your knees."

When Corrie thought about undressing and wearing one of Sam's shirts, she felt all goose-bumpy; the reaction wasn't from being outside.

After Sam brought her the towel and laid the shirt on the sofa, she rubbed down Jasper but she could feel Sam's attention focused on her.

"What?" she asked, looking up from her crouch next to the dog.

"I'm just thinking about you being a mother."

She felt her cheeks go warm. Was he going to say yes? "And?" She prompted.

He looked uncomfortable and she saw an expression

cross his face that she couldn't read. It looked like sadness. Maybe something even deeper than sadness. "I think you'll be good at it."

His words should give her confidence. They were a compliment. But she sensed something was troubling him and she didn't know what it was. She wasn't sure they knew each other well enough for him to confide in her. Did his thoughts have something to do with Alicia? Promises they'd made…hopes they'd had?

She'd come to Sam because he had so many qualities she admired—compassion and gentleness at the top of the list. He really was wonderful with his nephew and seemed to like children as much as animals. That's why she'd imagined he might be open to this idea.

Suddenly Sam muttered in a low voice, "Being a mother is a twenty-four-hour-a-day job."

She sank back on her heels and let Jasper run off with Patches. "I know that."

"Some women don't realize how much of a commitment that is. I guess that's why they get depressed after they have a baby."

"I know how much of a commitment motherhood is. I watched my mom raise me by herself after my dad divorced her. I know firsthand what being a single parent is all about." She also knew what betrayal was all about and infidelity and a man's inability to keep the most important promise he'd ever made. When she looked at Sam and felt a pull toward him, she had to remember that. She had to remember that attraction didn't go very far, and neither did the first couple of years of wedded bliss. All she had to do was envision her mother's tears and she could separate Sam the father to be, from Sam the attractive hunk.

"My parents divorced, too," Sam admitted. "But my dad raised us. My mother walked out because she wanted other things. Having a family was a commitment that took too much out of her. I guess what I'm saying, Corrie, is that you have to be absolutely sure about this, sure it's what you want. If you make this decision, you can never go back."

"I'm not impulsive, Sam," she argued, while at the same time realizing how hurt Sam must have been by his mother leaving.

He came a few steps closer to her. "It's just with this, the idea might be a lot more rewarding than the actual reality. Having a baby isn't easy and raising one is even harder."

"I can't let fear hold me back from doing something I've wanted my entire adult life. Sure, I love animals, but I want *kids,* Sam."

His brows quirked up. "Kids?"

She sighed. "I'll start with one then go from there."

"Do you know how much it costs to raise a child nowadays?"

She put her hand up in front of her and almost touched his chest. Almost. "Stop! Just stop. I didn't come here to ask your permission to have a child. Whether you're willing to donate your sperm or not, I'm going to do this. It's not a debate, it's a dream I'm going to make come true." She rarely showed her temper to Sam, if ever, but he was making her mad—as if he knew best…as if he were so much more experienced.

Although she thought he might back away, he didn't. He studied her with his steady brown eyes and she felt all trembly inside. She just wanted his sperm. She didn't want to feel…attracted. She didn't even want to think about them parenting together. She knew she couldn't count on Sam, just as she couldn't count on any male. She'd thought he'd be good father material, but who actually knew? *She* was going to be the constant in her child's life. *She* was going to make the important decisions. If Sam was the father, well, she'd just see how much he'd stick around. But the bottom line was, she didn't expect him to.

Because looking into Sam's eyes gave her an almost breathless feeling, she snatched up his shirt from the sofa. "I'll change."

His smile was mischievous. "Don't you want supper before you turn in?"

She felt like a fool. "I'm really not hungry. I'll change and then just curl up on the sofa." Under the afghan. So Sam's eyes on her wouldn't make her feel self-conscious.

Sam nodded to his bedroom. "You can sleep in there if you'd like, but it will be warmer out here if I keep the stove stoked. The sofa's lumpy—"

"The sofa will be great."

He looked amused again. "It's your choice."

She'd rather be warm than sleep in Sam's bedroom. If she slept in Sam's bedroom, she knew exactly what scenes would invade her dreams. She wanted no part of imagining him in bed with her. The reality of Sam Barclay was much different than daydream musings she might have entertained while working for him. She wanted to have his baby but in a *non*personal way.

Getting personally involved with Sam would be much too dangerous to her heart.

Chapter Two

The door to Sam's bedroom opened.

Corrie sat up, keenly aware of his presence.

"Getting cold?" he asked, his gaze taking in her tumbled curls.

"A little." He wasn't wearing a shirt, just gray sweat pants. Her eyes followed the curly path of his chest hair down to the drawstring. She jerked her gaze up to his eyes again.

In the hushed shadows of night and the silence broken only by the snores of the dogs cuddled in the dog bed beside the sofa, something primitive and powerful vibrated between her and Sam. Because it was the middle of the night? Because he was shirtless? Because she thought he was the sexiest man she had ever known?

Breaking the spell, he turned away from her and went to the fireplace. "I'll have this stoked up again in a minute."

She couldn't unglue her gaze from his bare back, his muscled arms and shoulders. "Do you cut your own firewood?"

"Whoever uses the stove has to replace what they burn. So, yes, I've been using and replacing since I've been here. Why? Are you interested in learning how to split logs?" He glanced over his shoulder at her and his smile was teasing.

"Hardly. I probably couldn't even handle the ax."

"I know for a fact you're stronger than you look. You lifted Mr. Huff's basset hound. He had to weigh fifty pounds."

After Sam closed the door to the woodstove insert in the fireplace, he brushed his hands against his thighs.

Corrie's stomach grumbled and Sam heard it. "You've got to be hungry. You hardly ate any supper."

That's because she'd felt like an idiot. After she'd taken Sam's shirt and changed in the bathroom, she'd returned to the living room realizing the darkness outside didn't mean it was time for bed. She'd been so rattled by their conversation and just being alone with him, that she'd forgotten all sense of time and place. He'd warmed cans of soup. Wrapped in the blanket on the sofa, she'd eaten some, just praying the hours would pass quickly.

While she'd leafed through magazines, Sam had worked at his laptop. Later he'd insisted he take the dogs out. It had been too cold and too snowy for them to stay out long and within fifteen minutes, they were all getting ready for bed.

"How about cookies and hot chocolate?" he asked her now, looking like a kid who knew better but wanted to have a treat anyway.

"We really *won't* get any sleep."

"No, but our sweet tooth will be satisfied and I bet your stomach will stop growling."

The room was warming already. Letting the blanket fall, she stood. She hadn't taken off her socks. She felt a bit ridiculous with his shirt on, which stopped just below her knees, and her knee socks which came up to her shins.

"I'll help you."

In the small kitchen, they couldn't turn around without bumping hips, rubbing elbows or standing practically toe to toe. She put two mugs of water in the microwave while he pulled the bag of cookies from the back of the cupboard.

The silence between them grew too full of everything they were both thinking and not saying. Corrie asked, "Did you really come out here to stoke up the stove?"

"I knew the cabin would get cold if I didn't, but… My mind won't stop circling around what you asked me. I mean, it's not like I'm dating you and one night foolishly we're not protected and suddenly we're having a baby. That's altogether different from what you're planning."

"Don't you see, Sam, this is so much better than the scenario you just described? We're both deciding if this is what we want. We're planning. If you were to tell me you don't want to be involved at all, that would be fine. I'll take full responsibility for this baby. That's what I want."

He studied her with an intensity that made her uncomfortable.

"What?"

"I don't understand why you're so set on taking this on alone."

"Alone isn't so bad. Alone, I don't have anyone else to answer to. Alone, I can make decisions for my child based on what I think's best. Alone, I don't have to worry about what someone else is going to do or say or think."

"Where does your independence come from, Corrie? What happened to you?"

His question took her aback and she couldn't just laugh it off. But she couldn't confide in him, either. They didn't know each other that well. "I told you, my mom and dad divorced."

"There's more to it than that. You're a caregiver. You don't hesitate to jump in and take care of a sick animal, to keep someone like Shirley company when she was lonely. What made you this way?"

If she clammed up and shut down, Sam would just turn away from her request as if it was a whim on her part. After thinking about Sam's question, she finally answered, "When my dad left, my mom and I took care of each other. She was a very loving person and didn't hesitate to help someone else when she could. I guess I just picked up on that. When she got sick—" She hadn't meant to say that. She hadn't meant to go into that.

The microwave beeped and she was glad for the interruption. Turning, she took the mugs of hot water from the small oven.

But Sam was right there, snagging the mugs from her, setting them on the counter. He towered over her while his bare skin, his male scent and his muscled arms seemed to surround her. "When did your mother get sick?"

"Oh, Sam. I don't really want to—"

He clasped her shoulders and looked deep into her eyes. "Tell me."

"I had graduated from college and was in my second year of veterinary school when she was diagnosed with ovarian cancer. She had no one but me. So I quit school to move back home and take care of her."

"That's why you didn't finish?"

Corrie nodded, a huge lump in her throat, not because she had to quit school, but because she still missed her mother. She could feel the heat of Sam's hands through his flannel shirt. She wanted to reach out and touch the stubble on his jaw. She wanted to let him hold her until his strength became hers and the missing and the loneliness went away.

"Why didn't you go back?"

She remembered how her mother wouldn't take any help from her father. They had both cut him out of their lives because he'd hurt them so badly. When a girl saw her dad with another woman, when he seemed to care more about that woman than about being a father and a husband, the pain of rejection cut deep. He'd made half-hearted attempts to see Corrie after he and her mother divorced, but Corrie hadn't wanted to see him. The visits had been too awkward because Corrie had just wanted him to go away. Except, she really hadn't. She'd just wanted her dad back—the dad he'd been before she'd caught him with a woman who wasn't her mother.

"I didn't go back to school because I'd used up my money paying for nursing care for Mom. I'm saving again. I'm still hoping to finish."

"And if you have a baby?"

"I don't have all the answers yet, Sam, but having a baby doesn't mean I can't finish school some day."

He released her shoulders and stepped away, putting more than physical distance between them. "Better mix in the chocolate or the water will get cold."

She wasn't sure what had just happened, but something had. She might not be the only one unwilling to confide her secrets.

When they'd settled on the sofa, Patches raised his head but then went back to sleep, his nose close to Jasper's.

"I'm surprised he doesn't mind sharing his bed," Corrie noticed.

"Patches never met a dog he didn't like."

She laughed and the tension that had cropped up between them dissipated.

Sam dipped his cookies into his hot chocolate and didn't seem bothered when they disintegrated in it. She took hers apart, licked off the icing and ate one half at a time. As she did, she noticed Sam watching her.

She wiped her hand across her mouth. "Crumbs?" she asked.

"A few." His voice was low and husky. With his thumb, he wiped the corner of her mouth.

She went very still. Time seemed to stop. Her breathing became shallower and faster.

Sam set his mug down on the coffee table. "I think I've had enough. I'm going to try to sleep again. You should, too."

If she slept, she knew what fantasies would invade her dreams—Sam kissing her...Sam making love to her.

Indulging in fantasies would throw her off course. She wouldn't let a man do that to her.

She would stay on course and become a mother—with or without Sam Barclay.

Sam came in the front door, the morning light brightening the cabin. The dogs followed him inside, and Corrie realized she hadn't even heard them leave. Sam looked different this morning and she noticed why—he'd shaved off his beard.

"I'm going back to Rapid Creek with you today," he announced. "I'll follow you."

She'd never expected this. "I didn't think you'd come home until the end of the week."

"I'm not sure the snow's finished. I don't want to see you get caught in it alone while you're trying to drive home."

It seemed Sam Barclay had a chivalrous streak. She should have known that but it had never been directed at her before. "I don't need your protection, Sam. Really. I'll be fine if you want to stay."

"It's time for me to go back. I'll be packed in about a half hour." Sam was keeping his distance this morning. She thought about last night on the sofa when he'd touched her so gently, so sensually, so temptingly.

"Have you made a decision about…anything else?"

"You'll be the first one to know when I do."

She felt herself blush. This new awareness between them was unsettling. It could be exciting, but she wouldn't let excitement take hold, not with what they were considering. She needed Sam as a friend, not as the hunky object of a teenage-like crush. Hormones as an adult were still hormones. She could control them as she always had. She'd never understood women who found themselves in situations they couldn't handle. Her mind had always ruled her body and she didn't see that changing now.

Corrie picked up the towel she'd used on Jasper last night. "I'll rub him down and then get a quick shower if that's okay."

"That's fine. Just don't stay in too long or you'll run out of hot water."

"Do you happen to have a hair dryer?" She thought he might laugh at her request.

Instead he frowned. "As a matter of fact, I do." His voice went lower. "I brought Alicia up here once and she forgot it."

Alicia. Alicia had been here with Sam.

Corrie knew without a doubt that the two of them hadn't slept in separate rooms. Alicia Walker was the kind of woman who went after what she wanted and she'd wanted Sam. Corrie still didn't know who'd broken the engagement but from the expression on Sam's face, now wasn't the time to ask.

Sam didn't stay while she toweled Jasper. Apparently mentioning Alicia had brought up memories he didn't want to think about. Maybe *she* was the one who had broken it off and he still wanted to be engaged. Maybe he still wanted to marry her.

When Corrie stepped into Sam's bathroom, she realized it wasn't as warm as the living room and she didn't dawdle in the shower. She'd forgotten to ask for a fresh towel so she pulled Sam's from the rack. It smelled like his soap and him. He rarely wore cologne. He'd told her after she'd been hired that some animals were skittish about smells.

After she vigorously toweled her hair and knew she wouldn't be able to do anything about the ringlets without a curling iron, she began dressing. She'd snapped her jeans and just fastened her bra when there was a knock on the door. She froze.

"I have the hair dryer," Sam called from the other side.

"Just a minute." Quickly she tugged her sweater over her head and lifted out her wet hair. As she opened the door, she was breathless.

Sam's gaze lingered on her wet hair. "You look different." He handed her the hair dryer.

"Just wait. I'll look like a dandelion gone to seed when I dry it with this."

He laughed out loud. "Corrie, I should have talked to you about more than animals the past couple of years. You know how to laugh at yourself. Do you know what a rare quality that is?"

"I just say the truth before someone else can. It's a defense mechanism."

"Maybe it is." As if he couldn't help himself, he reached out and tugged a strand of her hair that had gotten caught under her sweater and freed it to lie on her shoulder. He looked as if he wanted to say something…or do something. His dark-brown eyes were unreadable, but she thought he leaned toward her just a bit. Then he was stepping back.

"Thanks, I'll be finished in about five minutes," she murmured.

"We'd better get going as soon as we can. I don't like the looks of that sky."

Fifteen minutes later, they were on the road. Jasper and Patches had chosen to hop into Sam's van so Corrie led the procession, her mind racing. Would Sam decide to be her donor? And if he was, what then? Maybe both of their lives would be a lot simpler if she just went to a fertility clinic in Minneapolis. There was a good one there. Sam would be off the hook and she—

She just didn't like the idea of being impregnated by

a stranger's sperm. Sam's child… She smiled. Sam's child would be a handful, she was sure.

Snow began to fall, big heavy flakes mixed with shards of ice. The roads were plowed but not altogether clear from the day before. Corrie glanced in the rearview mirror. Sam was concentrating on the space between their cars. She felt so pleased he'd decided to follow her. She had lived in Minnesota all of her life and wasn't a stranger to driving on snowy roads. But the ice chips mixed with the snowflakes had her easing her foot off the accelerator and made her fingers grip the wheel tighter.

Corrie saw the mound of snow too late. The pile could have fallen from a vehicle as it was driven down the road. Wherever it had come from, as soon as her left front tire hit it, she went into a skid. Her anti-lock brakes kicked in but the car just wouldn't stop coasting. She ended up with her left side in the snowbank across the road from where she should be. The snowbank went halfway up her window.

It all happened so fast, she was almost dizzy with the speed of it. Her side of the car tilted into the snowbank and she couldn't see anything. She knew she had to get out and tell Sam she was okay, but she was still a little breathless from the skid—

The passenger-side door opened. She could hear barking—Jasper's shorter barks and Patches's more resounding ones. In an instant, Sam was inside the car, his voice worried, his expression set in stone.

"Corrie, don't move. Just tell me if anything hurts."

Hurts? She couldn't be hurt. She'd simply crossed to the wrong side of the road. She was wearing her seat belt and reached to unfasten it. "I'm okay. I feel so stupid—"

He stayed her hand. "Trust me a minute. Take a deep

breath." He was studying her—her head, her face, her neck, her shoulders, her arms. "Can you move your legs okay?"

She wiggled her feet, then moved one leg at a time. Brushing his hand away from the seat belt, she unbuckled it. "I'm fine, Sam, really. I'm not a china doll."

"Sometimes adrenaline kicks in after an accident. You can be hurt and not know it. Just sit still a minute."

So she sat, turned to look at him, and gave him a weak smile. "It's the car I'm worried about. Thank goodness the dogs were with you."

"They're having a fit. They wanted out of the van, but I just cracked a window. I need to know whether to call 911 or the towing service."

"My seat belt kept me safe. Really."

She turned her head from side to side and rolled her shoulders. "Everything works."

"Think you can slide across the seat so you can get out?"

"Sure."

He gave her another worried look then climbed out.

After she managed to transfer from the driver's seat to the passenger seat, Sam offered his hand to help her out of the car. She took it and it felt so big and strong and warm. As soon as she was on her feet, he was holding her at her waist. His face was close to hers, their breaths mingling white in the cold.

"Are you dizzy?"

Any lightheadedness she might be feeling came from being this close to him, not from running into a snowbank. She shook her head.

All at once his arms went around her and he pulled her in for a hug. "When I saw your car fishtail— Jeez, you scared me."

His head dipped a little closer to hers. She raised her chin. Their lips clung and held. Their New Year's Eve kiss had been impulsive, exciting, so filled with sexual chemistry it had scared the living daylights out of her. But this kiss…

It was hungry, passionate, all-consuming…

Suddenly it was over and Sam was shaking his head and swearing. "I'm sorry, Corrie. I—"

He was sorry? "Why?"

"Because you were just in an accident. I was more panicked than I wanted to be. We were both reacting. It wasn't…real."

Not real? That kiss had been real to her, but Sam obviously wasn't looking at it the same way she was. He clearly didn't want to admit there was any attraction between them this time any more than he'd wanted to recognize it after their first kiss. She couldn't let on how much it affected her…how much she'd wanted it. How very right it had seemed.

"If you don't want it to be real, then it wasn't real. It never happened," she stated matter-of-factly as she dug into the pocket of her jacket and pulled out her cell phone. "I'll call the auto club. I'm afraid we're going to be stuck here for a while."

"We can sit in the van," he assured her, his words even and tempered as she speed-dialed the auto club.

Forty-five minutes later, the tow truck arrived and pulled her car out of the snowbank. The mechanic looked over it and said, "I don't think you should drive it. The tire isn't flat but it could be punctured by the rim. The car's definitely out of alignment. We need to check that axle, too."

"We're headed for Rapid Creek," Sam said. "Can you work on it tomorrow?"

"Not likely. There were three other accidents. First come, first served. It will probably be Wednesday until I get to it."

Corrie felt as if she were going to cry and knew that was a ridiculous reaction. There had been a palpable tension between her and Sam as they'd waited in his van. A different kind of tension than after their New Year's Eve kiss.

They were still an hour from Rapid Creek. The tow truck had come from Calumet, fifteen minutes west of where they were now. "I can do without the car. I can walk to work. But I'll have to find someone to drive me to your garage when it's finished."

"I'll drive you back up here," Sam said firmly. "Is there anything you need in your car before he takes it?"

Since she'd already snagged her purse, she shook her head. "No."

"Then sign right here," the mechanic said, offering her his clipboard. "Make sure you give me a phone number where I can reach you."

Corrie jotted down her home phone as well as her cell phone number. Five minutes later, she was inside Sam's van again with the dogs in the backseat.

At first they'd barked and licked and made sure they'd gotten her attention. But after a few pets, scratches and a "We're going home now" they'd settled down. She, however, hadn't settled down. Beside Sam in his vehicle, she was too aware of what had happened between them. Too aware that this was a one-sided attraction and if she didn't call off the sperm donation, she'd be headed for...heartache. Whether she had a crush on the man or simply growing feelings for him, either would lead her down a painful road.

The snow finally stopped falling as they reached the outskirts of Rapid Creek. Sam had been silent during the drive until he pulled up in front of the apartment complex where she lived. "Are you still feeling okay?" he asked gruffly.

"I told you. I'm fine."

His frown deepened. "I'm going in with you."

"Sam."

"I'm going in with you. You can move around a bit, feed Jasper, just make sure all your parts *are* working okay."

Rolling her eyes, she unbuckled her seat belt and climbed out of his van. Sam opened the back door and called for the dogs. They followed them up the curved path to the complex. Jasper ran inside the town house and danced around the kitchen until Corrie filled his food dish. Sam kept an eagle eye on her while Patches sniffed everything in sight. She wouldn't have minded that eagle eye if he'd been watching her for something other than symptoms from the accident.

"Do you always keep your place this straightened up?" he asked.

She wasn't a clean freak, but she was neat. She had tidied up before she'd left for his cabin. "I usually put things away after I use them." Her voice was a little more clipped than it should be, but she was tired, feeling the effects of the drive and everything that had happened, not to mention not getting much sleep last night.

"Is there anything you need before I go?"

She approached him, looking him squarely in the eye. "I don't need anything from you, Sam. That includes your sperm if you have the slightest hint of a doubt about donating it. I only asked you because I thought it would be…easier. But now I'm not so sure. So whether you do it or not doesn't really matter. I'll have a baby with or without you."

She knew that look. The hollow in his cheek twitched just a little and his brow creased. He was keeping his temper in check. "I'll give you my answer in a few days. Do you want me to pick you up for work tomorrow morning?"

"That won't be necessary."

After a long look at her, he headed for the door but he stopped with his hand on the knob. "If you get a headache or you feel dizzy, I don't care who you call, but call someone. Promise me that."

She was an employee of his and in that respect, he did care. "I promise," she said solemnly.

Whistling for Patches, Sam left with his dog and shut the door behind him.

Corrie sank down to the sofa, laid her head back against the cushion and wondered what in the world she'd gotten herself into.

Chapter Three

Sam didn't like the way he'd left Corrie's town house yesterday. He didn't like it at all. And when she came into the clinic this morning…

Corrie was usually high-energy, efficient movement, cheery brightness. He'd always taken those qualities for granted. Today when she entered through the back door where he and Eric were talking about their schedule for the week, she gave them a smile that didn't quite come off as a smile, waved, said hi then went into the small lounge next to the kennel where she usually hung her coat.

Eric exchanged a look with Sam. "I wonder if she had a late night. Did you see those shadows under her eyes?"

Eric prided himself on being a connoisseur of women. He dated as many different ones as he could. Sam didn't know if Corrie had had a late night last night but he did know she'd been in an accident yesterday, and he wasn't going to go into a long explanation about that with his partner. He was worried. She looked pale and those circles under her eyes were dark. As he was about to go into the lounge to check on her, the receptionist, Jenny Newcomer, came in. She was fifty, loved animals and ran the office efficiently.

"Heads up," she said now. "Two Dobermans are on their way in. Is Corrie around?"

Corrie reappeared in the doorway to the lounge. "Jenny, could you pull their charts for me? I'll put them in exam room two."

Sam said, "I'll get them," his gaze still on Corrie. She looked tense. Was this all because she wanted him to be a sperm donor? Maybe they just needed a little conversation.

As she was about to go to the reception area, he clasped her elbow. "I took Patches over to Nathan's this morning because I knew I'd be busy catching up all day. Did you leave Jasper at your place?"

"Yes."

Her voice didn't sound as strong as it usually did when she continued, "I'll go home at lunch to let him out. That's the routine I followed while you were away. I hope that's okay. Eric didn't seem to mind."

"That's fine. Your lunch break is your own. Are you—" He didn't get the chance to finish as two Dobermans entered the reception area, barking for all they were worth.

Corrie took that opportunity to escape Sam's prying eyes and motioned to the dogs' owner to follow her to the examination room.

When Sam took over a few minutes later, Corrie slipped away as if she didn't want to be around him. That bothered him.

Midmorning, Sam entered Tabitha's examination room. Tabitha was a twenty-pound yellow tiger cat who was here for a general checkup including clipping her nails and a rabies shot.

"I'll get her weight," Corrie assured him as she began to lift the cat from her carrier.

Sam was about to ask Mrs. Clemson, the owner, a few questions when he heard Corrie's exclamation, saw her wince and quickly let go of the animal.

"Corrie?" He knew he sounded worried, but he couldn't help that. He went around the table, took her by the arm and led her outside the room. Over his shoulder he told Mrs. Clemson, "I'll be back in a few minutes."

"What's wrong?" he asked Corrie once they were standing in the hall.

She was really pale now.

"Don't tell me nothing," he warned her. "You're *not* fine. I want to know what's going on."

When she turned away from him, he laid his hand on her shoulder and squeezed gently.

The spark of defiance was gone when she finally replied, "When I breathe— I woke up around 4:00 a.m. and I just felt…bruised. Each time I take a breath it hurts. Not a lot, but when I went to lift Tabitha, I really hurt."

"I'm taking you to the emergency room."

"Sam—"

"No arguing. You were in an accident yesterday and I should have made you get checked out then. Go sit in the lounge until I talk to Eric and call Doc." Sam and Eric had bought the practice from Doc Merkle. Retired now, he helped them when needed.

"But what if it's nothing?"

"If it's nothing, Doc can go back home when I return. Go sit and I'll be there as soon as I can."

Fifteen minutes later, Sam was ushering Corrie into the emergency room feeling panicked. He was regretting even more leaving her the way he had yesterday, though he tried to tell himself her symptoms hadn't appeared until the middle of the night.

Still…

It didn't take a man with a genius IQ to figure out that Corrie wasn't a woman who liked to be taken care of. She was obviously used to being on her own and didn't want to depend on him.

She proved that when the technician took her back to an examination room and she adamantly refused to have him accompany her.

So he waited—pacing, paging through a magazine, pacing again. He didn't like this churned-up sensation. He definitely didn't like feeling as if this were his fault somehow. He had patience but not an endless supply. He hated hospitals as much as the next person, but hated waiting in one even more. After an hour, he'd had enough.

When the coast was clear, he opened the door leading to the examination rooms. There were only five. Finally he heard Corrie's voice and he headed for number three. The rooms were more like cubicles and had curtains that slid across the front. Corrie's curtain was partially open.

Sam stepped into the room. She was dressed in a hospital gown and looked so fragile he wanted to go to her and put his arms around her. What an odd sensation that was! He just kept telling himself he cared about her because she was his employee.

"What's wrong with her?" he asked the doctor as they both turned to look at him.

Before Corrie could protest, he extended his hand to the doctor, read his name tag, and introduced himself. "I'm Sam Barclay. I was with Corrie yesterday when the accident happened."

The doctor shook Sam's hand, but Corrie was the one who spoke up. "I'm bruised from the seat belt. That's all. The doctor's going to give me something to relax the muscles and I'll be fine in a few days."

"She works for me and handles animals," Sam told the doctor. "Should she be lifting?"

Since the cat was out of the bag, so to speak, the doctor relented and explained to Sam, "She should take it easy for a few days. By the end of the week, she should be ready for normal activity. But if you really want my recommendation, I'd say wait until next week to lift any animals, and then not fifty-pounders."

"I can't take off all week," Corrie protested.

"Yes, you can. You have sick leave," Sam replied.

"But who's going to get the charts ready and weigh the animals and make sure you don't scare them to death?"

Seeing Sam's glare at Corrie, the doctor said, "The prescription will be waiting for you at the desk. As soon as you're dressed, you can leave. Stop there to check out." Then he left the exam room.

"Eric and I can manage for a few days. Stop worrying," Sam assured her.

He saw the rebellion leave Corrie's eyes and when it did, they became shiny with emotion. Going to her, he sat beside her on the examination table and wrapped his arm around her. "You're not superwoman, Corrie. You just need to rest for a few days."

She was looking down at her hands and he suspected why. Lifting her chin with his finger, he saw the tear running down her cheek. He didn't think twice about pulling her close to him.

As soon as he did, he knew it was a mistake. She smelled like peaches and vanilla. Her curls were silky against his cheek. She was a soft bundle of woman and he was getting turned on.

What had happened to him since Corrie had appeared at his cabin? He'd been a monk since August and had liked it that way. But now the heat rising from his body, the heat from Corrie's, the beating of their hearts that now seemed to be in sync totally unsettled him.

He stiffened.

She felt the reaction and pulled away.

Both of them were embarrassed.

Finally, she murmured, "If you leave, I can get dressed."

He left, relieved and yet let down at the same time.

On the way to Corrie's apartment, Sam stopped at the pharmacy to have her prescription filled. She didn't say a word from when they left the hospital to when they arrived at her town house. He couldn't tell if she was hurting that badly or just upset with the whole situation.

Jasper greeted her when she unlocked the door. Sam imagined she usually stooped down to pet and play with the cocker spaniel when she came home. To offer her an alternative, he suggested, "Go sit on the couch and he'll jump up beside you."

Corrie gave him a look that told him clearly she didn't

want his suggestions. But after she took off her coat, she sat on the sofa and he had to hide a smile. Corrie might be independent, but she was reasonable, too. That was good to know.

Why was that good to know?

He tucked that question away.

She looked surprised when he removed his jacket. "Aren't you going back to the clinic?"

"I'm going to make sure you have everything you need first."

"I *have* everything I need." Her voice was strained and he'd gotten the message she just wanted to be left alone. But he wasn't leaving the same way he had last night. Today he'd make sure she was taken care of before he went back to work.

He strode into her sunny yellow kitchen, noticing the philodendron on the windowsill, the gingham place mats on the table and the matching gingham curtains at the window. After he opened the refrigerator, he shook his head. Yogurt and lettuce. Not a great combination in his estimation. The rest of the shelves were bare. Checking her cupboards, he discovered Corrie only bought what she needed. There was a can of this, a box of that and nothing substantial. Her freezer held two frozen dinners. That wasn't food as far as he was concerned.

In the living room, he picked up his jacket. "I'm going to buy you some groceries."

"No, you're not."

Crossing to the sofa, he crouched down in front of her. Jasper had jumped down onto the floor and was now pattering around him as if he wanted to go out.

"First, I'm going to take Jasper out. That way you

don't have to. Then I'm going to the deli and buy you real food."

"Like the corned beef you like?" She wrinkled her nose. "Spare me."

"You've made it clear several times you don't think much of Reuben sandwiches. I get that. But they have great soups, their own baked turkey and an assortment of salads. I'll bring a little of each."

"It will just go to waste."

"Not if I eat lunch with you."

She turned questioning eyes to his, and her voice wobbled when she asked, "Why are you doing this, Sam?"

He could see she wanted a straight answer. The best he could come up with was, "I regret not taking you to the emergency room yesterday. I should have called emergency services after your accident. I let you convince me nothing was wrong—"

"Nothing *was* wrong," she reminded him. "At least nothing I knew about."

"You should have called me when you woke up and had trouble breathing."

Rising to his feet, he zipped up his jacket. "You're too independent, Corrie. If you're even going to consider having a child, you need a network of people around you who can help out. I've seen it with Nathan. Sure Kyle needs his dad, but he needed a mother, too, and now he has Sara. My dad is always on the sidelines helping out and so is Val, Nathan's housekeeper. I'm around when Kyle just wants to have fun, and Ben fills another spot he needs to have filled. We're all necessary. Kids thrive when a variety of people care about them, especially if they don't have brothers and sisters."

She looked down at her lap, then raised serious eyes to his. "You and I grew up very differently, Sam. I was a loner. Other kids made fun of my hair and my freckles so I concentrated on schoolwork. I found friends in books and my mom was my best friend. After my parents divorced, she worked overtime to supplement what Dad gave us. I took care of myself. Would I want my child to grow up as I did? Maybe not. But I learned self-sufficiency and that's a good thing."

He studied those freckles that other kids had made fun of. Reaching out, he dragged his thumb over them. She went still, and he saw that same awareness in her eyes that he was feeling.

Straightening, he commanded, "Come on, Jasper. Let's take a walk." Picking up the dog's leash on a table near the door, he attached it to Jasper's collar. "I'll be back in a little while and then we'll talk about what you really want for lunch."

Opening the door, he felt as if he were escaping from a powder-keg situation. One too many sparks and…what? He'd kiss her again?

When his imagination started running rampant, he gratefully let the January cold seep into him. Maybe he could freeze his libido into submission.

Sam walked into his brother's house two hours later as he always did…without knocking. This time, however, he didn't find Val in the kitchen cooking or Kyle in the living room playing with his fire trucks. What he caught sight of was Nathan and Sara on the sofa kissing. They were so absorbed in each other they didn't even know he was there.

He cleared his throat…very loudly.

They broke apart like guilty teenagers and both laughed as they spotted him.

"We should have locked the door," Nathan growled.

Sara rose to her feet first, her pretty face flushed. "Patches is over at the lodge with Kyle and your dad."

"It's early for you to be heading home for the day," Nathan remarked. "Or has Doc decided he likes working at the clinic again and you're going to shorten your hours?"

"No chance of that. I did have to call him today, though. Something came up and I had to leave for a while. I thought I'd take Patches back with me."

"Why don't I go get Kyle and Patches," Sara suggested, heading for the hook at the back door where her coat hung. She motioned to the canister on the counter. "Freshly baked oatmeal cookies are in there." She stopped in front of Sam. "I'm glad you're back in plenty of time for the wedding."

"Have you decided on a honeymoon?"

When Nathan and Sara had come to the cabin after the New Year to tell him their good news and their wedding date, they hadn't decided yet about going away.

"I made reservations in St. Cloud for two nights," Nathan explained. "We don't want to be away from Kyle any longer than that right now. He's still adjusting to having Sara as a mom."

"I'll be right back," Sara promised, opening the door. She blew Nathan a kiss and then was gone.

Nathan, looking happier than Sam had ever seen him, crossed to the counter and pulled out the cookie jar. "Interested?"

Sam was still worried about Corrie. He didn't like the idea that she was at her place alone when she didn't feel her best. "No, I'm fine."

"Turning down homemade cookies? What's wrong, Sam?"

"Nothing's wrong."

"Why did you need a few hours away from the clinic when you just got back?" Nathan asked, in that older-brother, I-want-to-know-everything tone.

"As I said—"

"Something came up…" Nathan filled in dryly.

"Yeah."

This morning, when he'd dropped off Patches, Sam hadn't gone into detail about why he'd returned to Rapid Creek before Friday, when he'd planned to drive home. He could spar with his brother and sidestep his questions, but there was no point in postponing the inevitable. Sam didn't keep much from Nathan or Ben and the same was true with them. They'd always been available for each other at the important times in their lives.

Unzipping his jacket, Sam shrugged it off and hung it around one of the chairs at the table. "You know Corrie Edwards?"

"Sure."

"She came up to the cabin on Saturday."

Nathan's brows arched and he waited.

"You're not going to believe this, but she wants to have a baby. She wants me to donate my sperm."

"You're not thinking about doing it, are you?"

Sam remained silent.

"Sam?"

"I'm not sure how to say this, Nathan. I don't want to compare my situation to yours, but you lost a baby when Kyle was born and I know *you* know how that feels."

Nathan's first wife had died in childbirth and Kyle's

twin had died with her. Colleen had had trouble conceiving. Although the couple hadn't known it at the time, Sara had been the one to donate her eggs to help them. Nathan had returned to Rapid Creek with Kyle to recover from his loss. But he hadn't truly recovered until Sara had come into his life this past November.

"You're talking about Alicia's abortion."

"Yeah, I am. When I found out she'd terminated her pregnancy— It just tore me up. That was *my* baby, *my* son or daughter."

"I do know how hard that must have been."

"Let's face it, Nathan. When our mother left, it damaged all of us in ways we didn't even know. We saw what it did to Dad but we were just as affected. Somehow you managed to forget about her. When you married Colleen, you picked a good woman, and now with Sara you've chosen wisely again."

"She's the best."

Sam knew Nathan meant that and he agreed. He liked Sara a lot. "I think you made up your mind that our mother was just one selfish woman who wanted a Ph.D., life in a big city and her future in England more than she wanted us. But Ben and I— I think we believe all women are like her—selfish, with their own agendas. I mean, why couldn't I see just who Alicia was? Why couldn't I see children were the farthest thing from her mind? Oh, sure, we talked about having kids and she said she wanted them someday. But to her someday was way off in the future and I didn't realize that. I picked someone exactly like our mother. I just can't see me ever getting married."

"So you're actually considering Corrie's idea?"

"At first I thought it was ludicrous. I thought she was

crazy to want me to father her child. But the more I think about it… I realize it would be a way to be a dad without all the complications of marriage."

Nathan was already shaking his head. "You might not have marriage complications, but there *will* be complications. It's hard enough to raise a child when two people are connected. Sara and I still have differences of opinion sometimes on what's best for Kyle. She's helping me see I've been way too protective. We keep reminding each other we're looking in the same direction. We both want what's best for Kyle. But for two people who are relative strangers to try to parent together—"

"You and Sara were strangers before November. If Corrie and I become friends, we'll be able to parent."

"Are you trying to convince me or yourself?"

"I just know the idea…appeals to me."

"So what was the emergency today? Why did you need time off?"

Sam told his brother about the accident and what had happened at the clinic this morning.

At his brother's concerned expression, Sam was quick to assure him, "She's going to be okay. The doc at the E.R. said the seat belt bruised her. I picked up groceries and lunch for her."

Away from Corrie now, Sam told himself he really wasn't attracted to her. He was just finally over Alicia and he was coming alive again with the realization he hadn't been with a woman for a long time. But when he closed his eyes, he saw those freckles on Corrie's nose. He remembered how her curls fell around her face. He recalled the sensation of holding her in his arms.

"So what are you going to do?" Nathan asked him.

"I'm going back to the clinic and concentrate on work. I won't do anything until I know for sure what I *should* do."

"That sounds reasonable, but I just want to warn you, Sam—when kids and women are involved, reason doesn't always do a whole lot of good."

That was something Sam could think about while he was figuring out whether or not he wanted to be a dad.

Corrie relaxed in her recliner, Jasper on the floor right beside her, the nightly news flickering on the TV. She should get up and let Jasper out, but her ribs hurt and taking deep breaths wasn't a whole lot of fun. The doctor had told her today would probably be her worst day. She hoped he was right.

She just hated the fact that Sam had seen her like this, had seen her helpless. She hated feeling that way, always had and always would. She'd been helpless to stop the string of events that had occurred after she'd found her dad being unfaithful. She'd thought about not telling her mother, about not ever, ever telling anyone. But her dad had admitted to his wife what had happened, and everything had gone downhill after that. Corrie had been helpless to prevent the divorce, to prevent her mother's sadness, to prevent the crumbling of the life their family had known. And in some way she'd felt as if it were her fault. If she just hadn't gone looking for her dad that day—

She'd also felt powerless when her mom was diagnosed with cancer. That had been the worst kind of powerless. By quitting school and taking care of her mom, she'd known she was doing something to help. She'd never regret those two years. Never. She and her mom had gotten closer than they'd ever been before.

Corrie's doorbell startled her and Jasper. On guard instantly, the dog stood at alert then ran to the door and barked. Corrie lowered the recliner's leg lift and went to the foyer to peer through the peephole.

It was Sam. Why had he returned? She certainly had enough food in the house now, thanks to him.

After she unlocked the dead bolt and the doorknob, she pulled open the door. Patches sat beside Sam's leg, his tongue lolling out of his mouth. She only had a glance for the dog. Sam looked serious but oh, so handsome. His hair had seen a day of disheveling. He often ran his fingers through it when he was working.

"How are you feeling?" he asked.

Instead of fighting against his concern, she answered honestly, "Like I want to curl up in a ball until I can face the world again feeling better."

At that he smiled. "I thought I'd check on you before I settled in for the night. I can take Jasper for a short walk."

"You don't have to—" She stopped herself. "Thank you. I'd appreciate that and I'm sure Jasper would, too. Come on in. Have you been at the clinic until now?"

As he followed her into the living room, she was aware of everything about him, from his hair dipping over his brow to his terrifically broad shoulders to his slim hips in jeans to his black-booted feet, which were very big. This was Sam and she didn't know why she felt so awkward around him, but she did. Maybe because he'd seen her in a hospital gown!

She sank down onto the sofa trying not to jar her ribs.

Sam frowned as he watched her. "Are you sure you're going to be okay by yourself here tonight?"

"I'm not by myself. I have Jasper."

He gave her a get-real look.

"I can sack out on your couch," he offered.

That offer was tempting. On one hand, she'd like to have him around. Yet, on the other, she'd probably rest a lot better if he wasn't here.

"Not necessary."

Opening his jacket, sitting down beside her on the sofa, he rested his palms on his jeans-clad thighs.

"You might want to get used to having me around," he quipped. Then, more seriously, he added, "Because I've decided to be your sperm donor. I want to be a dad to your baby."

Chapter Four

"Have you told anyone yet?" Corrie broke the silence between her and Sam as they sat in her obstetrician's office early Thursday morning.

On Monday night Sam had agreed to help her have a baby. Yesterday she'd gone back to work. But ever since he'd given her his answer, there'd been an awkwardness between them. Because they were entering uncharted territory? Because Sam might be having second thoughts? Because she couldn't sleep at night, considering the fact that if she used a stranger's sperm, the process could be a whole lot easier?

After a glance at a pregnant woman who seemed to be engrossed reading a magazine, and a look toward the receptionist behind the glass window who was busy typing on a keyboard, Sam leaned closer to Corrie. "I told Nathan I was considering donating my sperm."

"Let me guess," Corrie returned in the same low voice. "He didn't approve."

Sam's brows arched. "It wasn't that he didn't approve. He just wanted me to understand how complicated this could be. Even he and Sara don't always agree on what's best for Kyle."

"Nathan and Colleen tried in vitro, didn't they?"

Scuttlebutt in a town the size of Rapid Creek echoed from one end to the other. Even before Nathan had moved back to Rapid Creek with Kyle, the rumor that he and his first wife had wanted children badly but had had problems conceiving had made the rounds. Whether Galen, Nathan's dad, had told a friend and that friend had told someone else, it was common knowledge that Nathan and Colleen had used an egg donor.

In November, when Sara had suddenly appeared at Pine Grove Lodge and over Thanksgiving had become a long-term guest in Nathan's log home, the town had buzzed with the possibility that she was Kyle's mother. It hadn't taken long for the gossips to learn that she'd been in an accident, had a hysterectomy and had come to Rapid Creek to meet her son.

"Nathan and Colleen did use in vitro," Sam replied. "Do you want to go that route if you can't conceive from artificial insemination?"

"I have enough money put aside for three tries at artificial insemination, but after that—"

"I'm paying half."

Corrie's gaze met his. "Sam, you don't have to do that. This is my idea. I don't expect you to pay anything."

"I'm paying half, Corrie. End of discussion."

Corrie had always thought Sam was different from his

brother Nathan. He was definitely more sociable, more outgoing. Yet she was beginning to see he had the same deep-seated values, the same moral code and a definite propensity to want his own way when he thought he was right. If he paid for half, would he be proprietary toward her? Would he think he could tell her what to do?

Before she could protest again, the door opened and a nurse announced, "Corrie Edwards?"

"That's me," she said cheerfully. Glancing at Sam, she saw he looked as uncomfortable in her obstetrician's office as she would look in the tavern at Happy Hour. But he'd insisted on coming with her and talking to the doctor himself. Trepidation fingertipped her spine because she was beginning to understand that Sam was going to do more than just show up for the procedure.

Their elbows brushed as they walked down the hall and she felt electrified. She told herself the sensation was just nerves. It was from the anxiety of learning what was going to come next. She didn't like uncertainty, never had and never would. But this uncertainty would pass. The reward of a baby was well worth a few anxious moments.

Corrie had already had a complete examination and a few tests after she'd initially spoken to her doctor about having a baby. So the nurse led them to the very end of the hall where the doctor's office was located. With a smile she motioned them inside and then closed the door.

"It's good to see you again," Dr. Witherspoon greeted Corrie, standing. She was in her late forties with pixie-cut black hair salted with gray. Small wire-rimmed glasses sat on the bridge of her nose.

Corrie turned to Sam. "This is Sam Barclay, Dr. Witherspoon. He's going to be the donor."

After Dr. Witherspoon smiled at Sam and shook his hand, he seemed to relax a bit. With steady hazel eyes, Dr. Witherspoon studied them both. "Corrie, I know it's none of my business, but would you like to tell me what relationship you have with Mr. Barclay? It will help me when I'm explaining the details of this process."

Corrie glanced at Sam. "He's a…friend."

When Sam's expression didn't change and Corrie didn't elaborate, Dr. Witherspoon nodded. "I see. All right then, let me tell you the usual procedure. Mr. Barclay, you will need to have a general physical, blood work, that type of thing. We can do that here or you can go to your own doctor if you're more comfortable."

"I'll see my doc," Sam agreed.

"Corrie said she'd like to begin this process as soon as possible. Do you agree with that?" the doctor inquired.

"That's fine."

Checking her notes, Dr. Witherspoon laid her pen on her blotter. "Do each of you have a lawyer?"

"A lawyer?" Corrie asked.

"Yes. I would recommend that each of you see lawyers to draw up an agreement…to lay everything out in detail so there are no misunderstandings or problems later."

"That might be standard procedure for strangers," Sam interrupted. "But Corrie and I have known each other and worked together for a few years. I want to pay for half of the procedure, but other than that… We'll see if she gets pregnant before we take the next step. A lawyer makes the process oppositional. We're on the same side."

Dr. Witherspoon's brows drew together. "I still believe you need an agreement to spell out everything."

"Corrie and I are going to take this one day at a time

with room for flexibility. I can't sign an agreement now that will dictate I should have visitation rights twice a week! I understand Corrie wants sole custody. But if we're friends, if I'm going to be a role model in the child's life, I'll be around whether something I sign dictates it or not."

"Are you saying you wouldn't abide by an agreement?" The doctor cast a worried look at Corrie.

Sam shook his head. "I'm saying we can't predict the future and the only agreement I'll sign is to put a child's interests first."

"Corrie?" Dr. Witherspoon asked. "You have to decide—"

"I've already decided. I asked Sam to be the donor because he's a good man. We'll figure this out as we go. As Sam said, *if* I conceive, our child will come first."

The doctor sat back in her chair. "All right. But you will have to sign agreements that protect me and my practice. Understood?"

"Understood," they agreed in unison.

The doctor glanced down at Corrie's chart. "You'll be starting your menstrual cycle in a few days, correct?"

Corrie felt her cheeks redden. She just wasn't used to discussing this kind of thing in front of people—especially men. "Yes."

"Mr. Barclay, do you think you'll have a problem getting in to see your doctor quickly?"

"No. If I call when we finish here, I should be able to go in tomorrow."

"Wonderful. Corrie will monitor herself carefully using an ovulation detection kit. As soon as the hormone surge has begun, she must call me. We'll have a twenty-four-to-thirty-six-hour window. Do you understand that you'll have to drop whatever you're doing and come in for the insemination?"

Sam shot Corrie a glance. "The timing is that critical?"

"Yes, it is."

Corrie had the feeling Sam was going to be on the Internet tonight researching the artificial insemination procedure.

"When will we know if she's pregnant?"

"In about two weeks. If she is, terrific. But if she's not, we'll begin the next cycle right away, unless there's some reason you want to wait."

"I don't want to wait," Corrie assured the doctor.

"What's the success rate?" Sam wanted to know.

"Ten to fifteen percent. Everything depends on the two individuals involved, the quality of the sperm and the eggs as well as a little luck thrown in. Let's see what Mr. Barclay's tests show before we decide whether or not to use fertility medication to give Corrie the optimal chance of conceiving."

Of conceiving.

Corrie couldn't wait until she was pregnant, until she was round with baby, until she delivered that baby. As she turned to Sam, their gazes met, their eyes locked and her heart fluttered.

Where was Sam going to fit into all of it? A year from now, would he still just be her boss, or would he be involved in her life?

Twenty minutes later they left the doctor's office, both of them quiet until Sam asked, "Do you need to stop at your place to let out Jasper?"

"No, my neighbor's going to do it."

He nodded. "Then we'll head back to the clinic." He

took out his cell phone. "I'm going to call my doctor to make sure I can get in tomorrow."

Corrie hoped that was enthusiasm she heard in Sam's voice. Yet she didn't want too much enthusiasm, did she? Just how much did she *want* him to be involved?

As he'd said, they'd take one step at a time.

A few minutes later, Sam had scheduled an appointment with his doctor for the next morning at eleven o'clock. After he tucked his phone into his jacket pocket, he veered down the side street to the clinic and turned into the parking lot. Eric's car was the only one there.

Sam switched off the ignition, climbed out of the van and came around to Corrie's door. His old-fashioned qualities made her smile.

"What's wrong?" he asked.

"Nothing. I thought men opening women's doors was a thing of the past."

"Manners we all learned from my dad. They stuck." After she climbed out and he closed the door, he didn't move away from the car, just looked at her thoughtfully.

"Is something wrong?" she asked. They were standing very near to each other. The lines around Sam's eyes, as well as the set of his jaw told her he had something on his mind. Maybe the doctor's appointment had made everything too real. Maybe he wanted to back out.

"Sam, if you're not one hundred percent sure about doing this—"

"What makes you think I'm not sure?"

"You've been quieter than usual for one thing."

Again, he just studied her. "We have some practical issues to deal with. I don't know how quiet you wanted to keep this, but we're going to have to tell Eric, especially if we're going to have to suddenly run together to Witherspoon's office."

"I hadn't thought about that. I guess we will. Will you tell your family?"

"Nathan might let it slip to Dad. But I'm not going to bring it up again unless you get pregnant."

Today that seemed to be a very real possibility and she broke into a wide smile. "Oh, Sam, I'm so happy you agreed to do this. Thank you." Standing on tiptoe, she kissed him on the cheek.

Before she was flat on her heels again, his arms went around her. His eyes were intent on hers and she felt the heat that had seemed to generate between them since that day in his cabin. The coldness of the day didn't seem to touch her at all while she was enfolded in Sam's arms. And when he bent his head, when his lips settled on hers almost possessively, she'd never been warmer in her entire life. To say the kiss was sensual and encompassing wouldn't begin to describe it. As she parted her lips, he thrust his tongue inside her mouth and the world around them disappeared.

As quickly as they'd come together, Sam now broke away, breathing hard, releasing her. "I shouldn't have done that again," he muttered.

She vividly remembered his reaction the first time he'd kissed her. Not wanting a replay, she knew what she had to say. "We got caught up in the moment. No harm done."

He looked so relieved she wanted to cry. "Yeah, I guess we did get caught up in the moment. It's not as if—" He stopped. "We want to keep this simple…clean."

"Right. You're still on the rebound from Alicia. And the last thing I need right now is an involvement with a man when all I want to do is have a baby and raise it on my own terms."

His eyes narrowed. "Not altogether on your own terms."

Her worry meter started ticking again. "Sam, I'm going to have sole custody. The child will have *my* last name."

He raked his hand through his hair. "Right," he remembered. "If I have anything to do with this child, you simply want me to be a role model or a friend."

"Exactly."

"But you *will* be open to a friend's advice?"

"I'll always listen to good advice."

Just then the back door of the clinic opened and Patches came bounding out. He barked when he saw Sam and ran to him, batting his long tail against Sam's leg.

Eric called from the doorway, "I thought you might want to take him for a walk. Ten minutes until our first appointment."

"I'd better go in and make sure everything's ready," Corrie murmured, eager to escape the aftereffects of their kiss.

Sam directed his attention toward the pine trees at the back of the property, then swung his gaze back to her. "Sara and Nathan are getting married Saturday night. Would you like to go with me?"

The invitation surprised her. "Are you sure they wouldn't mind? I heard the invitation list was small, just for friends and family."

"You're a friend. You're *my* friend."

Even though they'd kissed, she wasn't sure she and Sam *were* friends. But they'd better become friends because the process they were going to embark on could be embarrassing if they weren't.

"If I go with you, the gossips will start buzzing."

"They're going to have a lot more to buzz about if you get pregnant. Have you thought about that?"

She had and she told Sam the conclusion she'd come to. "The gossip simply doesn't matter. Having a baby does." Suddenly she decided, "I'd like to go with you to Sara and Nathan's wedding."

Sam nodded, she smiled and neither of them knew what to say next. She solved the problem by walking to the clinic while Sam took Patches for a short run. She wished…

She wished *nothing* where Sam Barclay was concerned. She just hoped his sperm could fertilize her egg. That's all she cared about.

A little voice in her head whispered, *You care about* **him,** *too.*

But she didn't listen to the whisper.

Tears welled up in Corrie's eyes and she was so embarrassed. She turned her shoulders away from Sam and faced the church aisle more squarely. The swelling organ music, the candlelight flickering, Sara—Nathan's bride-to-be—looking so beautiful in her Cinderella-type gown with its pearls and embroidery had caught Corrie off-guard.

Sam nudged her elbow and handed her a tissue. "Are you a closet romantic?" he asked, his voice very close to her ear.

Taking the tissue, she caught a tear, but answered him truthfully. "I might *want* to believe in marriage, but I know it doesn't work." What she meant was, *I know men don't know how to be faithful.*

"If the expressions on their faces is any indication, maybe Sara and Nathan's marriage will be successful."

Yes, Nathan's face said he adored Sara, and Sara's

gaze was so full of love Corrie could feel it where she was standing. But what would happen in three years or five years or seven years?

Galen, Nathan's best man, and Joanne, Sara's maid of honor and a close friend, looked on as Sara reached the altar. After Nathan lifted her veil, she took his hand. They faced the minister and Corrie could almost touch the tangible bond between them.

As she sat beside Sam, she listened to the minister's words, which held so much meaning, listened to Sara and Nathan's voices, which were so strong and sure.

Suddenly, Sam nudged her. "Your purse is vibrating," he whispered.

She'd laid her small clutch bag between them on the pew and she thought it would be a barrier, though albeit a flimsy one. She'd switched her phone onto vibrate even though she hadn't expected it to ring.

Unzipping the leather purse that matched the navy dress she'd worn, she slipped out the phone and opened it, recognizing the number immediately.

"Do you need to take it?" Sam whispered so near her cheek, she could feel his warm minty breath.

She swallowed hard. "No, it's my father. I'll handle it after the ceremony."

Sam gave her a questioning look. "Are you sure?"

She nodded. Sam had such a strong relationship with his dad and his whole family that he'd never understand how she and her father did and didn't communicate. Their conversation always seemed forced. Since her mother had died, there was even more strain between them.

Corrie's attention returned to the ceremony as Sara and Nathan motioned to Kyle, who had been sitting with Ben on the other side of Sam, to join them at the altar. She'd never seen anything like that before, but as the minister blessed the three of them, announcing them a family, she felt tears burning in her eyes again. This time she managed to blink them away.

After Nathan hiked Kyle into his arms and folded his arm around Sara, as they walked down the aisle happier than Corrie had ever seen a family look, a far-off dream nudged her. But she pulled a screen over it, knowing happily ever after was just an illusion.

A short time later, Corrie was seated next to Sam at one of the long tables in the church's social hall.

As Nathan guided Sara to an empty space in front of the food table for their wedding dance, Ben crossed to Sam and clapped his shoulder. "It all went off without a hitch. Now maybe we can get some sleep tonight."

Sam laughed. "I slept *last* night."

Ben shook his head. "Dad was roaming his place all hours, making a list of everything he had to do. And what's up with him and Val? He told me they're driving to the Wisconsin Dells together come spring."

"Nathan didn't tell you? They're officially—" he made quote marks with his fingers "—'seeing each other.'"

Ben looked astonished. "As in dating?"

"Yep. I think Sara had something to do with it. Before Christmas, she persuaded Val to get her hair cut, do some makeup, ask Dad to dinner. Dad seems happy."

"Sara played matchmaker?" Ben asked.

"I think she'd be proud to admit it," Sam said with a smile. Changing the subject, he asked his brother, "Are you still coming over tomorrow so we can make model airplanes with Kyle?"

"Yeah, sounds good. I have briefs to go over in the morning, but I'll come over around noon. We can make hot dogs and then put the kits together." Ben nodded toward Kyle who was sitting on his grandfather's lap, his head against the older man's shoulder. "He's tuckered out."

Sam glanced at his watch. "It's past his bedtime. As soon as Nathan and Sara finish their dance, I'll gather him up and take him home."

Transferring his attention to Corrie, Ben smiled. "Sam tells me you're as good with the animals at the clinic as he is. That's high praise."

Sam had introduced Corrie to his brother earlier in the evening when they'd arrived at the church. Whenever Ben flew into Rapid Creek, he only stayed a few days and she'd never met him before. "Sometimes I find animals a lot easier to deal with than people," she admitted.

Ben laughed. "I know *exactly* what you mean."

After a glance at the newlyweds, Sam gestured to them. "I guess that's as good a way to end a dance as any."

Sara and Nathan were kissing now and seemed oblivious to their guests. Although the music had ended, they were still in each other's arms.

Corrie felt as if she were glimpsing a much-too-private moment and she turned again to Sam. "Kyle's going home with you tonight?"

"Yep. Nathan asked him if he wanted to stay with me or if he wanted to stay with Ben and Dad." He grinned like a kid. "It was a tough choice but he picked me. I think Patches was the determining factor, though. I'm really glad his asthma doesn't kick up around dogs."

Corrie's purse began jiggling on the table.

Sam nodded to it. "Maybe your dad's calling again."

Opening her purse, she slid out her phone and opened it. "I'd better take this," she murmured, getting to her feet.

"I'll walk out to the lobby with you. I have to transfer Kyle's car seat from Nathan's SUV to my van."

Once in the lobby, Corrie answered her phone, which was on its fourth ring. "Hi, Dad."

She crossed to a corner of the lobby to have a conversation she didn't want to have.

Sam reentered the lobby of the church's social hall and stopped when he saw Corrie huddled in a quiet corner, her phone in her hand. A frozen expression on her face impacted Sam and he didn't know why. For the past week the sight of her got under his skin. Was that caused simply by the idea that she wanted him to be the father of her child?

He was beginning to think it was more than that. Something about Corrie herself, the fire of her red curls, her very blue eyes and small determined chin now revved him up. Although her navy dress with its short jacket was conservative, the outfit fitted her nicely. She wore flat shoes, though, and he smiled. It was like Corrie to think of comfort first.

But she wasn't comfortable right now. He could tell that from her expression. Instead of rejoining the guests inside the social hall, he waited for her.

After she closed her phone and spotted him, she looked surprised that he hadn't rejoined his family.

"Is your father okay?" he asked.

"He's fine," she replied, then added, "We've been playing phone tag."

Something about the way Corrie said that gave Sam the feeling she might have been the reason for the phone tag, as if talking to her dad wasn't on her priority list.

"Parents get a little crazy when they can't get in contact with their kids. My dad made that clear when I was up at the cabin."

"My father asked me to come to Minneapolis for Christmas and spend it with him," she admitted. "But I didn't. Doc wanted to go away over the holiday so I told Eric I'd help him with the animals in the kennel."

Sam knew Corrie took her responsibilities at the clinic seriously. "Eric could have taken care of them himself."

"He made plans to be away Christmas night, so I said I'd cover."

"How often do you see your dad?" he asked.

"Not often. We don't…we don't really have anything to say to each other."

"That's a shame. With your mother gone…" Sam trailed off.

"My dad and I ought to be close?" She shook her head ruefully. "We haven't been close since—"

"Since your parents' divorce?" Sam's mother had defected but if at any time she had held out a hand to her sons, if she had invited them into her life, Sam knew he would have accepted any olive branch. It sounded as if Corrie's father was interested in her life, but she wasn't interested in his.

"You don't understand, Sam."

Her eyes held sadness and he was suddenly curious

about her life…her past. "What don't I understand? I know how tough a divorce is, especially on the kids."

"I caught him with another woman," she blurted out. "I walked in on them and—"

The memory of it still bothered her, he could see. "How old were you?"

"I was twelve. My mom was out. I was supposed to have swim practice after school but it was canceled. They were naked on the sofa, their clothes on the floor. In our house." She took a deep breath as she shrugged. "I've never been able to forgive him."

Sam knew if he touched Corrie, he'd want to bring her into his arms. The last time he'd done that, he'd wished he hadn't.

He could only imagine how what Corrie had seen had impacted her as a teenager. Was that why she wanted to have a baby on her own? To protect herself from getting hurt as her mother had? That would surely make sense.

"Sam!"

The sound of his name startled him. Glancing over his shoulder, he saw Ben motioning him to come into the social hall again.

"Corrie, you, too," Ben called. "Sara's going to throw the bouquet and Nathan's going to toss the garter."

"Oh, I don't want to…" Corrie began.

Sam snagged her hand. "Come on. It will be fun. We can't break tradition."

Corrie gave him a weak smile. "No, we wouldn't want to do that."

In the social hall, the single women were already lined up around Sara. Sam hung back as Corrie reluctantly walked forward to stand a good two feet behind the cluster of single women. The eager women were huddled and she obviously wasn't eager.

But none of them had counted on Sara's great throwing arm. Even over her shoulder, she managed to toss the bouquet high and it practically fell into Corrie's arms.

Corrie looked as surprised as everyone else.

A cheer went up and the guests clapped. She raised the bouquet high like the sport she was and wiggled it.

Sam had to smile.

There were fewer single men than single women—about seven in all. Ben stood to one side of the group, Sam to the other. Nathan grinned. He made a great show of turning around and shutting his eyes but the garter headed like an arrow straight for Sam. It dropped at his feet and he had no choice but to pick it up. No one else was even close.

A round of applause went up. Sam caught Corrie's eye and slowly walked toward her. "What do you think?" he asked.

Taking a step closer to him and keeping her voice low, she murmured, "I think this proves we should have a baby together. We're meant to be partners."

He laughed heartily. Any other woman would expect a date out of the occasion serendipity had handed her. Corrie, however, always practical, had found a way to turn something romantic into a bona fide affirmation that they should go ahead with their plans.

He liked Corrie Edwards. In fact, he was beginning to think he liked her a little too much.

"Corrie! Sam!" Ben called from the podium where he was using the microphone. "Sara informed me there is a tradition we have to uphold."

Nathan had already picked up a chair from one of the

tables and positioned it in the empty floor space where the single men and women had gathered.

"Oh, no," Corrie protested. "We aren't really going to—"

"Yes, we are," Sam grinned as he urged her toward the chair. "Remember? We can't ignore tradition."

The expression on Corrie's face was priceless. She definitely did not like being the center of attention and Sam found that refreshing. Alicia had always wanted everyone's eyes on *her.*

Why was he making comparisons?

Sara took Corrie's bouquet, her eyes twinkling. "I'll hold this for you."

"You're enjoying this a little too much," Sam said in a low voice only his sister-in-law could hear.

She tapped the garter in his hand. "And you're not?"

The truth was he *was* enjoying himself…with Corrie.

From the mike, Ben said, "We should have a drumroll. But since no one brought a drum…"

The crowd began clapping rhythmically.

Corrie had seated herself in the chair and looked as if she wanted to disappear.

Leaning close to her, Sam assured her, "I'll make this quick. We'll be back at the table eating wedding cake before you know it."

Sport that she was, she gave him a wobbly smile.

Going down on one knee before her, Sam slipped off her shoe. Suddenly the crowd receded and when he gazed into Corrie's blue eyes, the world as he knew it shifted. As he took her foot in his hand, he saw how small it was, how feminine. He wished it wasn't encased in nylon. He wished he could trace his fingers up her bare shin.

Arousal hit him hard. Sucking in a lungful of air, he slipped the garter over her foot.

"All the way!" one of the guys shouted.

"Above the knee," someone else called.

As Sam moved the garter upward, he was aware of the curve of Corrie's calf, the tautness of her muscles. She was tense. Because of embarrassment? Or because he was touching her?

He shot her a quick glance. Their eyes locked, and he wished he could read her mind.

Although he'd told her this would be over with quickly, the garter caught below her knee. His fingertips lingered longer than necessary as she lifted the hem of her skirt and he pushed the blue lacy band to her thigh.

Finally the applause and cheers penetrated, and he hurriedly released the garter and rose to his feet.

When he offered Corrie his hand, she took it. With a nonchalance he didn't feel, he asked, "That wasn't so bad, was it?"

Corrie's cheeks were flushed, her eyes bright. "I'm just glad you're the one who caught the garter."

Because she felt comfortable with him? Because they knew each other?

To his dismay Sam realized he wanted Corrie to *like* him touching her. He wanted her desire to flare as his did.

Then he pushed that longing aside. Being a monk kept him out of trouble.

Wasn't life easier if it was trouble-free?

Maybe. But did he really just want "easy?"

He'd answer that question when Corrie wasn't around…when he didn't wonder if undressing her could turn him on as thoroughly as slipping a garter up her leg.

Chapter Five

Sam understood exactly the responsibility he'd taken on as first Nathan and then Sara leaned inside his van and kissed Kyle good-night in the car seat. "I have his inhaler, his medication, his favorite book and a kitchen stocked with all his favorite foods. Enjoy your honeymoon and don't worry. We'll be fine."

Corrie came running out of the social hall, carrying the bouquet she'd caught but also a small paper bag. Smiling at them all, she handed the bag to Sam. "These are the cars Kyle brought with him. They were on the table where he was sitting."

"Thanks, Corrie. Sam would have been back here at midnight looking for them," Sara joked.

Nathan added, "Although he seems sleepy now, I've got to warn you—until you get him to your place and dress him for bed, he might be wide-awake. Sara's been sitting with him until he falls asleep. We're not sure that's a good idea—"

"Nathan's indulging both of us," Sara added with a smile.

"They're making up for lost time." His brother's voice was a little husky.

Sam looked from his brother to his sister-in-law. "Go on your honeymoon."

"You have our cell phone numbers?" Sara asked.

"I do," Sam replied patiently. "Go. And be careful driving."

After hugs all around that included Corrie, too, Nathan wrapped his arm around his new wife and guided her to his SUV where someone had attached a Just Married sign to the rear window.

Peering into the back of his van, Sam saw that Kyle was dozing. He took the bag of cars from Corrie and noticed the long camel coat she wore over her dress. She was sleek and pretty.... He had to admit he'd enjoyed her company tonight, more than he'd enjoyed anyone's company in a long while.

She looked hesitant for a moment before asking, "Do you want me to drive over to your place with you and help you put Kyle to bed?"

They'd decided to drive to the church separately since Sam would be taking Kyle home with him.

"Do you want to practice?" he teased.

She seemed embarrassed that he'd guessed her reasoning. "Why not?" she asked with a sheepish smile. "I haven't had a lot of experience with kids and any would help."

More seriously, he considered her suggestion. "If he's missing Sara, having you there could ease him into his stay with me."

"All right. I'll follow you."

By the time Sam had carried Kyle up the stairs to his apartment, his nephew was more awake. "Do I have to go to bed now or will you tell me an animal story?"

Patches greeted them and Kyle leaned over Sam's arm to pet him.

"No stories tonight. It's way past your bedtime. We'll save them for tomorrow."

Corrie had carried in Kyle's small duffel.

"Can you find his pj's in there?" Sam asked her.

She went still and her gaze came up to his; her eyes seemed to mist over.

This time, Sam could read her mind. They could be having this conversation about *their* child someday— someday soon if all went well.

Corrie broke eye contact first and unzipped the duffel while Sam carried Kyle down the hall. Ten minutes later, he was fetching a requested glass of water. Crossing the threshold into his spare bedroom, he stopped. Corrie was kneeling before Kyle, nimbly fastening the buttons of his pajama top. Sam could so easily see her as a mother. She might not have had much experience with children, but she was a natural.

After Kyle scrambled up onto the bed, he sat cross-legged. "Can Patches sleep with me, Uncle Sam?"

"I don't think that bed's big enough for you *and* Patches."

"Maybe Uncle Sam will let you bring Patches's bed in here so he can sleep *beside* your bed."

"Can I? Can I do that?"

"I suppose you can. But I should take Patches outside one last time first."

"Corrie can stay with me. Maybe she knows a story."

"You have to go to sleep," Sam protested.

"I won't fall asleep until Patches is sleeping, too."

Sam knew that was probably true. "I'll be back in five minutes so the story has to be a short one."

"I'll tell him all about Mrs. Timberlake's cat and how she climbs up the curtains," Corrie offered.

Kyle looked entranced by that idea.

Sam had just reached the doorway when Kyle asked him, "Is Corrie your girlfriend?"

Glancing at Corrie's expression, Sam could see Kyle's question had made her as uncomfortable as Sam felt. "No, she's not my girlfriend. We're just…friends."

Kyle looked perplexed. "But Corrie's a girl and she's your friend, so she's a girlfriend."

"He's got you there." Corrie's eyes twinkled as she sat down on the bed beside Kyle. Then she explained to the five-year-old, "For some reason, if you say I'm Sam's girlfriend, that would mean we have special feelings for each other, like your mom and dad have. If you say I'm just Sam's friend, then that means we get along and like some of the same things. It's weird, but that's the way it is."

"You both like animals," Kyle concluded as if he'd just figured out why they were friends.

"Exactly." Sam finally felt as if he was off the hook.

As he stepped into the hall, Kyle called after him, "My mom and dad were friends before they got married."

With that declaration hanging in his apartment, Sam beckoned to Patches and went outside. When he thought about kissing Corrie, he knew they had more than animals in common. They had chemistry. But he also realized they both had walls built around their hearts. Obviously with Corrie it seemed her childhood had affected her deeply…deeply enough that she had trouble believing men could be faithful. As for Sam, Alicia had broken his trust and he wasn't over that yet. He wasn't over losing their child.

As far as he and Corrie were concerned, friends were all they could be.

Corrie didn't know if Sam expected her to leave right away…or stay! As he said a last good-night to Kyle, she sank down onto the sofa thinking about the bridal bouquet in her car.

Coincidence. Sheer coincidence.

A few minutes later, Sam joined her in the living room. He'd unfastened his black tie and tossed his tuxedo jacket over a chair. With a beard line starting to shadow his jaw he looked rumpled and sexy. Her heart raced and her stomach felt jittery.

"All tucked in?" she asked, just to make conversation, just to take her mind off the attraction to her boss that had plagued her from the day she'd started working for him.

"He's asleep. He could hardly keep his eyes open to say good-night."

Sam lowered himself to the sofa beside her, his thigh brushing hers.

She swallowed hard.

"He likes you," Sam said.

"I like him." Kyle was very easy to love, and she knew her heart was ready to love her own child.

"Every time I take care of him, I admire Nathan more. I know after Colleen died, he wanted to hole up in a cave and never come out. But he moved here and started a new life, making Kyle the focus of it. I've never seen Nathan as happy as he was tonight. Sara has…I don't know… brought him alive again."

"Both people have to be willing to compromise to make marriage work. It's obvious Sara loves Nathan. And Nathan, well, he seems like the faithful type."

Sam studied Corrie for a very long moment. "Men *can* be faithful."

"Do you really think so?" She asked the question without cynicism.

"I know you have doubts because of your dad, but all men aren't like him."

Actually, Corrie didn't want to believe they were, but Tom… After dating him for a few months, believing they were totally in love, he'd walked away into the arms of someone else. Corrie had always felt *she* was the one who'd been lacking. Having sex with her had been based on a dare. He hadn't been serious at all from the get-go.

"Why are you looking so sad?" Sam asked.

"I'm not—"

His palm cupped her chin and her whole body quivered from his touch. "You don't hide your feelings well."

"I'm not an open book," she protested.

"We all have secrets that eventually come out."

She didn't have secrets, just confidences she didn't easily share.

The hum of the refrigerator was the only sound in the apartment. Sam's dark-brown eyes were so gentle and compassionate, she could almost blurt out her life's story. They were caught in a freeze-frame. That gentleness in his eyes became something else entirely.

When he murmured her name, she could have melted. She leaned forward, hardly an inch. His hand slid from her jaw to her cheek and she could feel the erotic roughness of calluses. She imagined his fingertips other places....

He swore as if he knew he shouldn't kiss her again but couldn't help himself. She couldn't help herself, either.

This kiss was harder, more demanding than the others. He didn't wait for her lips to part but slid his tongue between them as if he had the right.

She could resist. She could stop. But this was *Sam*. She inhaled his scent, recognized his taste, and felt herself falling into desire that was exciting...exhilarating... totally new.

"She is your girlfriend or you wouldn't be kissing her!" a surprised little voice chirped from behind Corrie.

Sam broke the kiss and Corrie couldn't wait for his explanation to Kyle...because she wanted to hear it, too!

On second thought, maybe she didn't.

Rising from the sofa on shaky legs, she turned to Kyle and explained before Sam could. "That was just a goodbye kiss. It's time for me to go home to Jasper."

"Is that a dog?" Kyle asked, his eyebrows furrowing.

Hoping she was steadier than she felt, Corrie went to Sam's kitchen table and picked up her purse. "It sure is. I've been taking care of him for a while. He gets lonely without me."

Then, before Kyle could ask more questions and before Sam could give weak explanations that she'd rather not hear, she put on her coat and crossed to the door. "You have a good time with your uncles tomorrow," she said to Kyle with a smile she dredged up from somewhere. To Sam who'd narrowed his eyes and was watching her escape as if he didn't approve, she suggested, "We'll talk at work on Monday." With a little wave, she slipped out the door.

Inhaling a deep breath, she realized she was still trembling inside from the aftermath of Sam's kiss. She may have had a crush on him for a couple of years, but now she was beyond a crush. She was falling for him, fast and hard.

She had to stop the fall before she landed and broke her heart. She wanted a baby, *not* a lover.

That's what she told herself the whole way home.

Sam had just finished an annual exam on a rottweiler Tuesday afternoon when his cell phone vibrated. Deciding to take the opportunity to grab a cup of coffee, he answered the phone and went to his office. "Sam Barclay," he greeted the caller.

"Sam, it's Dr. Weigel."

Sam stilled, knowing exactly what this call was about. Before last week, he hadn't given a second thought to physicals and sperm counts and motility. After all, Alicia had gotten pregnant. But tests were tests and he'd always wanted to pass them with flying colors.

"How am I, doc?"

Dr. Weigel was in his early sixties and had cared for Sam and his brothers since they'd entered high school. He was one of those old-time doctors who believed if he got to know his patients, then that knowledge would help with diagnosis and recuperation. He knew the Barclay family well and acted more like a favorite uncle than an aloof professional.

"You're just fine, boy, in fact I wish I was as fine as you. In addition to general good health, your cholesterol is where it should be. You'll be getting an official report with your numbers in the mail. But I don't think it's your cholesterol you're worried about right now, is it?"

"You heard from Dr. Witherspoon?"

"Yep. The report came in about an hour ago. Looks like you're good to go. Your swimmers have pizzazz. I imagine you'll want to tell your lady friend right away."

The prospect of telling Corrie embarrassed him and that was absolutely stupid. Maybe if he hadn't kissed her. Maybe if the scent of her shampoo didn't drive him nuts. Maybe if the way she walked didn't turn him on.

"So you'll let me know if I should buy cigars?" Dr. Weigel joked.

"I'll let you know," Sam replied, the reality of going through with the artificial insemination hitting him hard. He could be a father soon. A father!

After he thanked the doctor for his call, he went in search of Corrie. He found her in the kennel, petting and talking to a calico cat they were treating. He closed the door behind him as he stepped inside. She turned to face him. "Do you need me out there?"

"No, there's a lull. My doctor phoned."

Her eyes were wide now with expectation. "About your tests?"

"Apparently I passed with flying colors. We're set to go. Your doctor will probably be contacting you."

Corrie's face absolutely glowed. "This time next month I could be pregnant! Oh, Sam." She threw her arms around him and gave him a hug. "I don't know how to thank you for doing this."

Roughly he muttered, "I haven't done anything yet."

As if suddenly self-conscious, she dropped her arms and stepped back. "I guess you're not as excited as I am."

"The impact is hitting me little by little," he admitted.

"Your life won't be changing substantially. Mine will," she reminded him.

"That's if you get pregnant."

"*If* I get pregnant," she murmured.

His mind suddenly filled with pictures—Corrie in late stages of pregnancy, Corrie holding a newborn, breast-feeding.

The door to the kennel opened and Sara stood there smiling at them. "Jenny said to come on in."

Sam's sister-in-law looked absolutely radiant. He imagined a honeymoon with the perfect partner could do that.

"Now that you're back and we're back, I wanted to invite you to dinner."

Corrie murmured something about leaving them alone to talk and was about to exit the room when Sara stopped her. "Why don't you come to dinner, too, Corrie? Kyle really enjoyed your animal story. He told it to us over and over again."

"I don't want to intrude on a family gathering."

"No intrusion at all. Galen and Val are joining us and *I'm* cooking for a change. I told Val she couldn't lift a finger. How does Thursday evening sound?"

Corrie exchanged a look with Sam as if asking his permission to accept. He found himself liking the idea of her having dinner with his family, seeing how she fit in. After all, his dad might become a grandparent again and would want to spend time with a grandchild.

"Why don't you come, Corrie?" Sam coaxed. "And bring Jasper so Kyle can meet him, too. He'll love running with Patches at Nathan's place."

Although Corrie still looked uncertain, she nodded to

Sara. "All right. Thank you. What can I bring? I make a mean batch of peanut butter fudge."

"Kyle will love that and so will Galen. He has a sweet tooth from here to next year. I know you never know when you'll get finished here, so why don't we say seven?"

Sam's life sure had taken an interesting turn since Corrie had driven to his cabin. He'd hardly thought about Alicia and what she'd done for the past week. He felt good about moving ahead with his life. And he was almost as excited as Corrie about what the next turn around the corner would bring. He could be a dad within a year.

A dad.

After dinner on Thursday evening, Sam's dad reached for his jacket on a hook by the door. "Why don't we take the mutts out for a run?"

If Sam had worried about Corrie fitting in he shouldn't have. As she helped Sara and Val clean up after dinner, she joined right in swapping recipes.

From his dad's expression, though, Sam knew he had something on his mind. His deepening friendship with Val?

Rapid Creek had been snow-free for the past week. Patches and Jasper chased each other down the walk and around to the back of the house.

Galen's breath puffed white in the night cold. "Are you and Corrie Edwards involved?"

As a father, Galen noticed everything about his sons. He was sharp and nothing passed by him unnoticed. The brothers didn't keep much from their dad but Sam was reluctant to tell him what he was planning.

"Why do you ask?"

"I just wondered if Sara was playing matchmaker again, or if there was a reason for her asking Corrie to dinner."

"I think she wants to get to know Corrie better. I imagine she misses her friends in Minneapolis."

"Maybe. She thinks Val and I didn't notice, but she made a few suggestions here and there that brought us together. I suspect she's doing the same thing with you and Corrie. You know, to help you get over that fiancée of yours."

His dad hadn't liked Alicia and never made any bones about that. He might as well tell his father what he was planning. He didn't keep secrets from his family. "Corrie and I are going into a…partnership of sorts."

"Is it something to do with the clinic?"

Patches and Jasper were now sniffing along the row of bushes and Sam kept his attention focused on them as he replied, "No, not about the clinic."

"Spit it out, son. What's so hard for you to say?"

His dad was a plain talker and never beat around the bush. Usually Sam appreciated that, but tonight…"I'm going to be a sperm donor so Corrie can try to have a baby."

Galen's jaw dropped as he gaped at his son. "You *are* kidding."

Now Sam felt defensive, and he crossed his arms over his chest. "No, I'm not kidding. I'll probably never get married, Dad. Alicia kicked one big hole in my ability to trust a woman."

"But what you're doing doesn't make any sense at all….unless you have an ironclad agreement spelling out what's going to happen. Are you planning to donate your sperm then walk away?"

Sam knew from his dad's tone he disapproved of that

idea. "No, of course not. I'll be a role model. I'll help Corrie make decisions."

Galen glared at him. "It's hard enough to be a dad when a man's married. It's twice as hard when he isn't. What you're doing here could hurt everyone. The baby Corrie wants to have, most of all. Have you thought this through?"

"Sure, I have. Corrie and I are reasonable adults."

"Reason doesn't enter into it. What if this baby gets attached to you and then Corrie marries someone else? What will you do then?"

"Corrie's not interested in marrying anyone, either," Sam muttered.

"She might say that now, but women have a romantic streak men can't even dream of. If the right man walks into her life, you'll be history."

The bitterness his dad had felt—and rightly so—about his wife walking away had never been completely resolved.

"Corrie would never keep me away from my child."

"You might think that now, but when things change in a relationship, a man can't know what a woman will do. You have to talk to Ben about protecting your rights, sooner rather than later, if you're going through with this."

"I'm going through with it."

"Then be smart about the decisions you make. You need everything spelled out in writing with both of your names on the dotted lines."

"We can't spell everything out if we don't even know if she's going to get pregnant."

Galen scowled. "Call Ben."

Over the weekend Sam had thought about talking through the situation with Ben. His older brother never hesitated to give his opinion or his legal advice. But Sam didn't really want to discuss this with him until he had all the issues settled in his own mind. For now, he and Corrie would deal with the insemination process itself. If and when she got pregnant, they'd take the next step.

Didn't that make the most sense?

Corrie had a great time with Sam's family but as he walked her out to her car and Jasper jumped inside, she knew something was on his mind. He'd been fine until he and his dad had taken the dogs out. Then Galen had looked at her…differently and Sam had gone quiet. She didn't need a sixth sense to know something had transpired between them.

Sam opened the driver's-side door for her.

"Something wrong?" she asked.

After a long look at her, he dug his hands into his pockets. "I told my father what we were planning."

"He had objections?"

"You could say that. He brought up some points I hadn't considered."

"Such as?"

"Such as the possibility of your marrying someone and leaving me out in the cold where the baby's concerned."

"That isn't going to happen. I told you, Sam, I'm just not interested in marriage."

"I know, but if the perfect man came walking into your life, what would you do?"

The perfect man. The perfect husband. There was no such creature. They all had agendas of their own. Men were goal-oriented, hunter-oriented. Even Sam. Though if she had to make a wish list of perfect men, his name would be at the top.

"Trusting is hard for me."

"Because of your father."

She nodded, letting it go at that. There was something demeaning telling him she'd been the butt of a frat boy's challenge.

"Why do you trust *me* then? It will take a certain degree of trust to do this. You know that."

"I've worked with you for three years. I see the way you run the clinic, have a partnership with Eric, how you deal with the animals and the other staff, even how you deal with Doc, your dad, your family. If I can trust anyone in this process, Sam, it's you. It's why I asked you. And I guess you're going to have to trust me to be fair about the baby, to let you into his or her life. We'll be able to work out the details. We *are* reasonable adults, aren't we?"

"I think we're becoming friends. Maybe that's more important than any other connection we can have."

Friends who kissed, a little voice reminded her.

She didn't take the reminder seriously. A kiss was just a kiss, a crush was just a crush. Falling for Sam was just an infatuation that would pass. The baby was the most important thing of all.

"Are you having doubts, Sam? Because if you are, we can call the whole thing off."

Stepping closer to her, seeming more like the old Sam, he smiled. "No, no doubts. My father is old-fashioned in the way he thinks, though he doesn't want to admit it. He doesn't realize that now there is more than one kind of family. Two parents and children could become obsolete. As you said, we've known each other for a while and lately I've watched *you* just as you've watched me. I wouldn't be doing this if I didn't think you'd become a good mother."

Sam's opinion meant a lot to her, maybe too much.

"So…I should start using my ovulation-detector kit?" she asked, the thought of doing it making her happy and warm all over.

"Yeah," he replied. "I'll be ready whenever you are." He gave her that crooked grin that curled her toes in her boots.

This was the old Sam, the Sam she'd known before Alicia Walker entered his life.

When Corrie slipped into the driver's seat, Sam didn't close the door right away. He hunkered down and kissed her on the cheek. She felt the touch of his lips all the way to the very deep places inside of her.

"Thank you, Corrie, for asking me to be a sperm donor. It's going to change both of our lives." He closed her car door.

Now all Corrie had to do was pray she got pregnant.

Chapter Six

"Sam, it's Corrie. I'm ovulating! I called my doctor and we're doing the insemination tomorrow morning."

As Sam heard the excitement in Corrie's voice on the last night in January, he got excited, too. This is what they'd been waiting for, wasn't it? "I'll call Eric so he knows we'll both be out of the office in the morning."

"Have you told him what we're doing?"

"Last week." Eric had given Sam a look that said, *What? You can't get laid and you have to become a dad this way?* But his partner hadn't tried to talk Sam out of it as his dad and Nathan had. He appreciated that.

"I'm not going to be able to get any sleep tonight," Corrie went on.

"Corrie, you know the percentages on this." She was so determined to get pregnant, so sure that this was the way her life should go. She would be let down terribly if it didn't happen.

"I just know this is going to work, Sam. I just know it."

"What time do we have to be there?"

After Corrie told him, Sam insisted he'd pick her up and take her to the hospital. When he hung up the phone, he felt different somehow…as if his life were going to start in earnest now.

Corrie felt…changed somehow. Did that sensation come from the fact that she could soon be pregnant with Sam's baby?

As she lay on the gurney, a sheet over her hospital gown, she felt such mixed emotions she didn't know which one was at the top of the list.

Was she *really* doing this?

There was a light rap on the door. "Yes?" she called.

Sam opened it. "Do you want company while you're waiting to be released?"

"Sure," she replied brightly, but the sight of him now made her stomach jump, her heart flutter and warm tingling invade her whole body.

Pulling one of the vinyl chairs over beside the gurney, he sat on it and joked. "You know, don't you, this would have been one hell of a lot cheaper and easier if we'd done it the old-fashioned way."

She felt heat start at her neck and creep up. "For you maybe."

The words had just slipped out and when she saw Sam's expression, she wished she hadn't said anything.

"What does that mean?"

"Nothing, Sam."

But he never accepted her evasive answers. He took her hand. "Tell me what you meant."

"You're going to think me really strange," she murmured, feeling so embarrassed. But this was Sam. She could tell him anything, couldn't she? After all, she'd told him about her father and she'd never told anyone about that.

He cocked his head and studied her. "*Strange* is not a word I'd use to label you."

She realized he really meant that. Even though she was sometimes in tune with animals more than humans and lacked an active social life, Sam accepted her just as she was. That's what she'd always liked about him—his acceptance of others.

Before she could formulate an answer to his original question, he asked, "Are you a virgin?"

She laughed a little, looked down at the sheet and pleated it between her fingers. "No. But I've only had sex once."

"Once?" Although he'd suggested the possibility of virginity, he still looked surprised at her answer.

"When I was in college, I was still idealistic, maybe even a romantic. I told myself over and over again that my dad wasn't the standard father and husband, that there was no reason that I couldn't take a chance on love and be happy rather than miserable like my mom had been. There was a man in my chem class who was a frat guy, great-looking and always seemed to be enjoying himself no matter who he was with. He'd missed class a couple of days in a row and asked me for my notes. We started talking and he asked me out. I…guess I wasn't your usual coed. We dated for a few months before I knew I was in love and decided to go to bed with him. In my mind, I was envisioning bridesmaids and a wedding veil. After that night, I learned the hard way that sex didn't involve commitment."

"What happened?" Sam prompted when she stopped.

"He didn't call for a week. At first I thought maybe he was just busy. I called him and left a message, but he didn't call back. That's when I began to realize something was wrong. We'd gone into the next term by then and I didn't have classes with him anymore. Ten days after our night together, I saw him with another girl, making out as if there was no tomorrow. I shored up my courage and talked to one of his frat brothers' girlfriends. She told me the reason he'd dated me wasn't that he wanted a relationship. He'd dated me because I was a challenge. Apparently I had an 'ice maiden' reputation and a few of his frat brothers were joking around one day saying no one could get to first base with me. He bragged that he could. And he did. I was a notch on his belt and then I was history."

Sam lifted her hand and held it between both of his. "I can only image how your self-esteem was affected by what happened. But that guy was an absolute jerk and what he did had nothing to do with *you*." He sounded as if he knew all about men and what they did.

"And how did you arrive at *that* conclusion?" she asked with a rueful laugh, the touch of Sam's skin on hers bringing back memories of his kiss.

"You weren't a woman to him, Corrie. You were a means for him to build up his reputation, a way for him to look good to his frat buddies. You're pretty and sexy. You're warm and funny and you care a lot. You've got to forget about what that guy did to you because *he* was the one with the problem, not *you*."

After a moment of thoughtful silence, he asked, "Is that the reason you haven't had sex again?" He pulled his hand away, and Corrie could still feel the warmth of his skin against hers.

"After that, I just felt that no man *could* be faithful. I mean, my mother thought my dad loved her. He married her, they had me, they kissed each other good-night, ate breakfast together every morning and then suddenly, he's in love with someone else! I could understand that maybe two people could grow apart, but he didn't talk about it with her. There had been no hint he was unhappy. Instead of separating, getting a divorce or even trying to put his marriage back together, he plunged into an affair."

"Did he marry the other woman?"

"Yes. He and his mistress were together a whole year before that didn't work out, either."

"Did he want to get back together with your mom?"

"I don't know. But she was so hurt, Sam, she didn't want him anywhere around. He'd broken her trust and she could never forgive him."

"And you saw it all."

"I saw it all. When Mom was diagnosed with cancer, I thought maybe she and dad would make peace. But he didn't come around and she never said she wanted him around. When he attended her funeral, I was just so angry at him… I blamed him somehow for all of it. I know that wasn't rational." She shook her head. "But deep down I believed that all that hurt Mom experienced just ate at her and it gave her the cancer that took her life."

After a few moments of thoughtful silence, Sam asked, "So you and your dad haven't made peace, either?"

"No. Avoiding him is easier than dealing with him," she answered honestly.

Sam didn't tell her she was wrong. He didn't tell her she should reach out to her father. Maybe because he realized she already knew that that would be the right thing to do.

This time the silence grew long between them, and Sam stood. "I think I hear Dr. Witherspoon out there. After I take you home—"

"I'm not going home. I'm going to work. She said I could resume my normal activities."

"Don't you think it would be better if you just take it easy today?"

"If I go home and lie on the sofa with my legs elevated, I don't think it will increase my chances of pregnancy."

"Are you sure?" he asked, arching a brow. "Sounds like a fun afternoon to me."

She laughed, too. When her laughter died away, she admitted, "I'm going to wait two weeks to have an official pregnancy test. I want to be sure."

Sam didn't have a chance to comment as the doctor pushed the door open. Dr. Witherspoon entered the room and Corrie realized that if she didn't get pregnant, she'd be heartbroken.

Twelve days later, Corrie was checking on the morning surgical patients when she felt the first twinge of a cramp. She knew her body well. When she ducked into the bathroom a short time later, she'd gotten her period.

Holding onto the sink, she stared into the mirror. *You didn't expect this to work on the first try, did you?*

Honestly, she had. It had seemed so right.

She had to tell Sam she wasn't pregnant.

He was in his office bringing charts up to date when she rapped on the door and went in. He had changed from his scrubs back into his jeans and chambray shirt. He checked his watch.

"First patient here already for the afternoon?"

She shook her head, not wanting to just blurt out the news that she wasn't pregnant, but not knowing how to work into it gradually. "No, no one's here yet. I…I…got my period. I'm not pregnant."

Rolling his chair back, he stood. "I'm sorry, Corrie. I know how much you want this."

"I have to call Dr. Witherspoon. I want to try again. Do you?"

After a moment, he nodded. "Yes, I do."

Coming closer to her, he clasped her shoulders. She wanted to rub her chin against the top of his hand, but the gesture would be too personal, too intimate, too more-than-friendly. For the past twelve days they'd gone their separate ways. They'd worked together but hadn't seen each other outside of the clinic. It had almost seemed as if Sam was careful not to touch her, not to get too close. But right now, she wanted him close.

"The first time is just a trial run. Think of it that way," he encouraged her.

She knew he was trying to help her put the procedure into perspective but she had to swallow hard and blink fast or her emotions would get the best of her.

"Oh Corrie, I know you're disappointed." Instead of just holding her shoulders, now he was pulling her to him, and she didn't want to be anywhere else but right where she was—in Sam's arms. She was almost afraid to breathe, afraid to move, because she didn't want him to pull away.

But he did pull away. "We could both use a distraction. How would you like to go to the Valentine's Day Dance the Ski Association is throwing."

"The Ski Association?"

"Yeah. They just built that new social hall over on Broad Street. They're having weekend dinners, that type of thing. Nathan has a batch of tickets to sell at the lodge."

"I don't know, Sam."

"It would be good for you to get out. You'll know Nathan and Sara."

"I'm not a recluse," she protested.

"No, but you put in long hours at the clinic and that doesn't leave much time for friends and fun."

Sam did have a point. There was only one thing that bothered her. He probably wouldn't be asking her to go if it weren't for this joint endeavor they were undertaking. If she hadn't asked him to be a sperm donor, they'd still be going their separate ways and the Valentine's Day Dance wouldn't be part of it at all. It wasn't going to be a real date. A real date happened when a man wanted to be with a woman because he liked her, was attracted to her, wanted to spend time with her. Sam, well, Sam was just being nice.

But if he was just being nice, would he have kissed her as he had?

Maybe they could have a good time together. In fact, maybe if she did some shopping, made an appointment with a hairdresser, maybe she could get Sam to see her as a woman, not a friend who wanted to have a baby. A real woman.

Looking into his eyes, feeling her heart jump when she did, she accepted his invitation. "I'd love to go with you to the dance."

She thought Sam might pull her into his arms again. She thought he might even kiss her. But the cell phone on her belt started to vibrate and when she looked down at it, he did, too.

"You might as well get it," he said gruffly. "You can take it in here if you want. I have to check my afternoon schedule."

Before she could ask what time he was going to pick her up on Saturday night, he was gone from his office.

Taking her vibrating phone from her belt, she saw her dad's number. An electrician, he made his own hours and apparently right now he was free. She could just let it go to voice mail, but she didn't. She pressed the green button and said, "Hello, Dad."

"Corrie? Are you busy?"

Her father always started off their conversations with that. He gave her an out if she wanted it. "I'm at work. The afternoon onslaught hasn't started yet so I have a couple of minutes." She checked her watch. It was noon. "Are you taking a lunch break?"

"Uh, I'm at home right now."

Something in the way he said it made her ask, "Are you okay?"

"Yes, I'm fine. I had to run a few errands so I took the day off."

There was a short pause. "I know how busy you are and that it's hard for you to get away. So after thinking about it, I decided, why shouldn't *I* come visit *you?*"

"Visit me?"

"Sure. My schedule's free the third week in March. We could have a *real* visit."

They'd never had a *real* visit. She wondered what this was all about. Maybe he was thinking about getting married again. "You'll be coming alone?"

"Yes, I'll be coming alone. As I said, I want to visit with you. If you don't want me to stay at your place, I can get a room somewhere. It would be a vacation for me. I could drive around the area, maybe go hiking."

"It's the dead of winter, Dad."

"Well, then, maybe I could learn how to cross-country ski."

Something was up. "Do you want to tell me what this is all about?"

"It's about me wanting to spend some time with you. I understand you have a job and a life, so you don't have to entertain me every minute I'm there. I might even do some ice-fishing. It will give us the chance to have a few dinners together or whatever."

She and her dad didn't spend time together well. There were always awkward silences and a strain that had been there since she was twelve. "Are you sure this is how you want to spend your vacation?"

"I'm sure, Corrie."

It only took a moment for her to decide the right thing to do. "All right. Of course, you'll stay at my place. It's silly for you to pay for a room somewhere when I have two bedrooms."

"We can start out that way. If I get in your way, I can take a room somewhere else. I hear there's a great lodge up there."

"Whatever you think is best, Dad."

Silence crept between them again until her father's voice grew gruff. "I want to get to know you again, Corrie. That's what I think is best."

She didn't have anything to say to that and when she clicked off a few minutes later, she wondered what had happened to her dad. Why had he finally decided he had to get to know his daughter?

The third week in March, she'd find out.

That evening, Corrie sorted through her closet looking for the perfect outfit for Saturday night. She pulled out a green dress with long sleeves and a flared skirt, held it in front of her and then asked Jasper, who was asleep on her bed, "What do you think?"

The dog opened one eye, lifted his head, sighed then put his nose on his paws again and went back to sleep.

"Oh, great. I guess that commentary means it's boring."

The truth was, almost everything in her closet was boring.

When she cast a glance down at her mostly utilitarian shoes, her doorbell rang. Seven-thirty on a Friday night. Who could that be?

Jasper perked up at the sound of the bell, jumped off the bed and went running down the steps to the living room. The dress was boring, but a guest wasn't. While Jasper barked, Corrie checked the peephole. To her surprise, she recognized Colin Bancroft—Shirley Klinedinst's lawyer.

Before she opened the door, she pointed her finger at Jasper and said, "Stay." He cocked his head but obeyed. When she opened it, Mr. Bancroft smiled at her.

"Miss Edwards. I hope I'm not disturbing you."

Colin Bancroft was in his early sixties and had always been very formal and polite with her.

"No, you're not disturbing me. Is something wrong?"

"Nothing's wrong. I just wanted to see how Jasper was."

"Come on in."

Once Mr. Bancroft was inside and the door closed, Jasper ran around him in circles, barking and greeting him. When the lawyer stooped down to pet him, Jasper licked his face.

"I can see you're healthy and happy." Jasper licked his face again and he laughed.

As Bancroft straightened, Corrie asked, "Can I get you a cup of coffee or tea?"

"No, nothing for me. But I have something for you." He motioned to her sofa. "May we sit?" He was carrying his briefcase.

Once they were seated, he opened it on his lap and took out a sheaf of papers. Jasper climbed up beside Corrie and settled in. She petted the dog while she watched Mr. Bancroft.

"Have you found a permanent home for Jasper?" she asked. Actually, she'd be sad if he had. She and the dog had bonded and it would be terribly hard to give him up. She could see that now. Maybe she hadn't spoken up soon enough.

"No. And I haven't for a very good reason. The past few weeks since you've cared for Jasper have been a test."

"A test?"

"Let me start at the beginning. Mrs. Klinedinst wasn't exactly what she seemed."

"I don't understand."

"Shirley lived meagerly in her farmhouse, but she didn't have to. Before he retired, her husband owned the hardware store in town and essentially had no competition. He saved his money wisely, invested it when lots of folks were just putting it into savings accounts. He sold out when a chain store started buying up old hardware stores in small towns. He made a wonderful profit. But when he retired, Shirley's arthritis kicked in and they didn't want to travel or buy a big car or move to a more modern house. They liked their life. They were happy with each other, and their investments kept accumulating. After Marvin died, even though Shirley's arthritis became more debilitating, she wanted to stay at the farm where all her memories were. She adopted Jasper and with help from people like you, she had a happy life."

"Mr. Bancroft, I don't see what this has to do with me."

"You were the only friend Shirley had who consistently cared about her and looked in on her. You brought her groceries when she needed them, you took Jasper to the vet for her, and you even arranged for her neighbor to take her to her doctor's appointments. I can't tell you how grateful she was for all of that."

The truth was, when Corrie had moved to Rapid Creek, she'd been lonely. She'd taken care of her mother for two years because her mother had needed her. In Rapid Creek, no one had needed her except for her furry patients at the clinic.

"Shirley told me over and over again the story of how she met you. She'd phoned the veterinary clinic when Jasper was sick but had no way to get him to the doctor."

"He'd gotten into a box of chocolates," Corrie remembered.

"Exactly. When you learned she had no way to transport Jasper to the clinic, you went and picked him up."

"He was one sick puppy."

"That he was. But you looked after him, the veterinarian made him well and then you took him home to Shirley's. She never forgot that kindness."

"She was a wonderful lady. I'd just lost my mother and missed her. I loved to listen to Shirley's stories."

"And she loved listening to yours. You brought the world in to her again. Because of that, I have an offer to make to you."

Corrie had no idea what was coming. Of course, she'd keep Jasper if that's what Mr. Bancroft was getting at.

"Shirley was a wealthy, wealthy woman. She had no family. These papers I have here are just the beginning of her legacy, a foundation for animals who need a home."

"What a wonderful idea!"

"I'm glad you think so because my instructions are to turn the farm into a shelter for homeless animals if you will run it. You will receive a yearly salary." He named a sum that was twice the amount that Corrie made now. "If for some reason you don't want to run the shelter yourself, you can still become its director, staff it and oversee it. Shirley trusted that you would hire the right people. As the director, you would also earn the same yearly salary. You would not have to be on hand on a daily basis, but you would supervise, organize, hire, fire and replace staff as need be. If you don't want to do either, I have orders to sell the property to a developer, give you a life-long stipend for Jasper's care if you choose to keep him and give the rest of Shirley's money to the Humane Society."

Corrie's head was whirling with everything Mr. Bancroft had told her. "How soon do I have to make a decision about this?"

"You can take your time. I can give you until April first. The only answer I need tonight is whether or not you want to keep Jasper."

"Oh, yes, I want to keep Jasper. There's no doubt about that. But the rest… I'm in the process of doing something that could change my life."

"As much as Shirley's offer could change your life?"

"Yes, just like that."

"I see. Why don't I let you think about it? If you have any questions, or if you want to discuss it further, you can call me at any time."

Corrie stroked Jasper once more and stood. "I miss Shirley," she said simply, her eyes filling with tears.

He patted her shoulder. "I know you do. You both loved animals and that's what brought you together. Just know that whatever you decide, one decision is not better than another. This is your choice, Corrie. Shirley didn't want this to be a burden, but a legacy and a new way of life for you if you want it."

"Thank you, Mr. Bancroft." She walked him to the door.

After she'd said good-bye, she watched him walk to his car. She should tell Sam about this. She should tell him about it right now.

Yet maybe she needed to think about it first. Yes, she needed to think about it. She needed to sort out her feelings. She needed to think about the baby they could have, and how a child would fit into the job of caring for homeless animals.

She doubted she'd get much sleep tonight. She had a whole lot of thinking to do.

Chapter Seven

Corrie opened the door to the Hair Hut Saturday afternoon, concentrating more on the offer Shirley's lawyer had brought to her than on what she wanted to do with her hair. How did this new opportunity fit in with having a baby?

What would Sam think if she left the clinic? Leaving might be the best option if she *did* get pregnant. She didn't want Sam always looking over her shoulder, did she?

Remembering Sam's caring attitude after her accident, she wasn't so sure.

The Hair Hut was busier these days than it had ever been. Last summer Ralph Durand from New York City had moved to Rapid Creek to get away from the rat race and had bought the salon. His schedule was usually filled three weeks ahead. He employed two other hairdressers and Corrie had made an appointment with Shannon who'd trimmed her hair before. Shannon had just swept the area around her chair and was ready for her. With a smile, she motioned for Corrie to have a seat. "Just a trim today?"

Corrie suddenly wanted more than a trim. She wanted Sam Barclay to notice her tonight…notice her as a woman. She took the band from her ponytail and let her curls tumble around her face.

"Actually I want more than a trim. And if I ask you what would look good on me, what would you do?"

Shannon's brows arched under her bangs as she narrowed her eyes. "I'd layer it and give your curls more freedom and movement, I'd also take it up a little bit, maybe an inch and a half. You wouldn't be able to tie it back in a ponytail any longer."

Corrie thought about it. "I can't have it in my face while I'm working."

"No problem there. I'll just give you bangs. With your high forehead, you can wear them. You'll have a totally different look."

Corrie thought about it for all of two seconds, then she agreed. "Let's do it."

Forty-five minutes later, Shannon finished with the diffused-air hair dryer, and Corrie studied her reflection in the mirror. "I like it."

"If you let it air-dry, you'll get the same look. If you want to use a hair dryer, you'll need the diffuser. Or you could use a curling iron to set your waves. You've got lots of possibilities. I'd love to have hair like yours."

"The grass is always greener," Corrie murmured, shook her head and watched the curls swing again. She looked different, more sophisticated…even sexy maybe?

Five minutes later, she was writing out a check when a woman appeared at her elbow and asked, "Corrie?"

Corrie wasn't shocked exactly but she was surprised to see Alicia Walker, Sam's former fiancée. The woman had been out of town since September. As a travel agent, she'd had the opportunity to work in one of her chain's offices in California. Corrie had wondered if she'd left because of her breakup with Sam, or if Sam had broken up with Alicia because she wanted to pursue opportunities elsewhere. This was one time when gossip hadn't had much to say because no one was talking. If Alicia had friends who knew the truth, they kept it to themselves, as had Sam's friends and family.

Corrie handed Shannon her check along with a tip, accepted her receipt, and turned to Alicia, feeling uncomfortable because the blonde had once been intimate with Sam. Corrie didn't like that idea at all. Her gaze slipped over Alicia's figure in designer jeans, a wide leather belt with a sterling-silver belt buckle, a snug black sweater and slim-fitting cropped jacket. She knew there was only one reason this blond beauty had stopped her.

Sam.

Still, she forced politeness. "Hello, Alicia. When did you get back in town?"

"On Thursday. I've just been catching up and getting my bearings again. How's everything at the clinic?"

"Everything's just fine. We're busy, busy, busy. Sometimes I don't even have the chance to eat lunch." She knew this wasn't what Alicia wanted to hear but she wanted to know what the other woman would say.

Alicia's smile slipped a bit. "I understand Sam was away for a while. That must have left you short-handed."

Oh, Alicia had been catching up all right. "Doc covered for him."

"How long was Sam gone?"

"Over the holidays." She didn't need to tell Alicia he was gone for Thanksgiving, Christmas *and* New Year's.

"I'm sure it was a well-deserved vacation. He always works too hard. Did he go far?"

"Up north," she said helpfully.

Now Alicia frowned. "I bet he went to his family's cabin. He took me there a couple of times."

Corrie specifically remembered what Sam had said, *I brought Alicia up here once.*

Once.

"Did you go ice-fishing?" Corrie asked ingenuously.

"Ice-fishing?" Alicia gave Corrie a sly smile. "We had better things to do than that."

That comment did it. Corrie tucked her purse under her arm. "I'd better be going."

"Tell Sam I said hello. In fact, tell him I'll stop in and see him one of these days and we'll…catch up."

Corrie didn't exactly remember pushing open the hair salon's door and walking half a block south before she realized she'd parked her car in the other direction. That woman had always gotten under her skin. What had Sam seen in her?

As soon as she asked the question, Corrie knew exactly what Sam had seen in her. Alicia Walker was five-ten with a luscious figure, beautiful brown eyes, wavy golden hair and a voice that was as smooth as silk. He'd seen a woman he wanted to take to bed and he'd done just that. Somehow he'd wrapped dreams of marriage around Alicia and he might have lived happily ever after with her.

Except…

Something had happened.

Whatever had happened didn't matter to Corrie. The fact was—Sam wasn't with Alicia now. Tonight he was going to be with *her*—Corrie Edwards—and she was going to make an impact. She loved her new hairdo, but she had to do more than get her hair cut to wow him. She hurried to her car. First she was going to stop at that little boutique that sold overpriced beautiful dresses. She'd have to find a sensational pair of shoes, too. The last stop before she went home would be the makeup counter of the department store.

Tonight Sam Barclay wouldn't know what hit him. Tonight, Sam Barclay would see her as a sexy woman.

Sam felt as if a wrecking ball had hit him. Standing in Corrie's living room, he couldn't think of one thing to say. Finally, he asked, "Corrie Edwards! Is that you?"

Even Jasper, sitting on the floor staring up at Corrie, knew his mistress looked different. Sam couldn't quite believe this was his vet assistant, normally seen in smocks and usually with little or no makeup. Corrie's hair was styled and silky, waving around her face in such a way that it enhanced her facial structure, her high cheekbones, the tilt of her nose, her small chin. Her blue eyes looked absolutely enormous. Her lashes seemed thicker and fuller. He could hardly notice any freckles, but her lips were coated with lipstick that looked wet.

His stomach clenched. His groin tightened. He realized how aroused he was becoming and they hadn't even gotten to dinner. She was wearing the kind of dress he would never imagine Corrie wearing. It was black velvet and it clung to her. The V-neckline dipped far enough that he could see the swell of her breasts. The long sleeves seemed as though they covered a lot of skin, but the skirt that draped to her calves had a slit up the side. That slit made a man want to see more.

He was so thrown off balance, he asked, "Can you walk in those shoes?" The heels had to be three inches high. The shoes' straps went from her toes up her ankle. Could a shoe be any more seductive?

"Sure, I can walk in them," she claimed as she crossed to the chair and picked up her coat.

When Sam saw the hole in the back of her dress, he almost broke out into a sweat. The way her tush moved... He wished he'd left the door open to let the cold air in. He rimmed his finger around the collar of his dress shirt, thinking about unfastening the top button.

"Am I too dressed up?" Corrie glanced at him innocently over her shoulder.

Somehow he found his voice. "No. No, of course not. This is probably one of the few dress-up occasions in Rapid Creek."

Corrie pointed to Jasper's bed on the sofa. "Come on. Jump into your bed."

The dog did, and Corrie hunkered down to pet him. "Stay out of trouble until I get home."

The dog barked as if in understanding and Corrie laughed.

At that moment, Sam had never seen a more beautiful woman—a woman he'd like to take to bed, a woman who made him feel as if he'd been in cold storage for too long.

"We'd better get going."

Sam took Corrie's coat from her arm and held it. It was dark-green wool. He realized he'd never seen Corrie Edwards dressed up like this before. She was a sight.

As she slipped her arm into one sleeve, he caught the
scent of perfume, sweet and musky. The dangle of her
onyx earrings caught in one of her curls. He slid his
thumb under it, releasing it. His face was so close to her
there was only a breath between them. "You look fantas-
tic tonight."

She smiled up at him. "So do you." Her eyes were on
his lips and he felt a rush of adrenaline surge through him
that he had to fight down.

He helped her into the other sleeve. "Let's go celebrate
Valentine's Day." He couldn't keep his arm from going
around her as he walked her to the door.

Sam felt the pounding awareness between him and
Corrie as he drove to the Ski Association, parked and led
her inside. He was acutely aware of everything about her
whenever he was with her, but tonight, with those dangly
earrings almost touching her creamy shoulders, her curls
a little bouncier, freer, softer, that dress whispering seductive invitations with the way she walked in it, he
wondered if he'd lost his mind or if his libido was simply
running rampant. Maybe he'd kept it in check for too
long. Maybe not having sex really could make a man
crazy. But then he thought about his father and all his
dateless years and he knew that wasn't so. Whatever was
happening was happening to him...only him.

Maybe his body merely wanted to prove he was over
Alicia and ready to move on to someone else. But was
Corrie that someone else? And did he even want to move
on? He didn't believe she was the type of woman who could
have meaningless sex, and that's all he wanted, wasn't it?

In the lobby, Sam took Corrie's coat and hung it on a
rack there. His hand landed on the small of her back to

guide her inside and his fingers met skin…bare skin. It was warm to the touch and he was on fire. He tugged his tie just a little.

When Sara spotted them, she waved and they crossed the room to join her and Nathan at their table.

"We saved you seats."

"I like your hair," Sara said to Corrie. "It looks great. Did Ralph do it?"

"No, Shannon cut it. I just told her to do something a little different."

Sam wondered why that was. Why was Corrie feeling the need to break her pattern? "That dress isn't like anything you've ever worn, either."

"Does that mean you like it?" Sara teased, giving Corrie a wink.

"Any man would," he responded noncommittally. He'd noticed men's gazes swing toward Corrie as she'd walked across the room. It had been an odd feeling. He'd almost felt…jealous.

Because she might become the mother of your child?

Yeah, probably that was it.

"Do you ski?" Sara asked Corrie.

"No, I never have. When I lived in the city, there wasn't the opportunity. Here, I've just never taken the time."

"We should have Sam teach you," Sara suggested. "He's an expert at cross-country. Ow!" Sara exclaimed and looked over at Nathan who had obviously nudged her under the table. She wrinkled her nose at him and he just shook his head.

Sam knew what that was about. His brother didn't think his wife should meddle, but Sara would always do what she thought best. Sam really didn't think she was suggesting anything romantic between him and Corrie. After all, teaching a friend whom you'd known for three years to ski was something that would be quite natural. However, the only thing that would seem natural between him and Corrie tonight was a kiss that could lead to bed.

Although the room had filled, Sam barely noticed anyone else at the dinner. Sara and Corrie talked as if they were old friends—about the owner of the hair salon, about the boutique where Corrie had bought her dress, about Kyle and school and Sara opening her own law office in Rapid Creek.

"Will you specialize in anything?" Corrie asked.

"No, I'm going to do a little bit of everything—wills, estate planning, maybe house settlements."

Corrie's gaze swung to Sam and he knew she was remembering the discussion about lawyers they'd had with her obstetrician. He supposed she was thinking he would have one in the family. He had two, actually, but Ben couldn't practice in Minnesota. He still didn't see the need for a lawyer. Unwise or not, he just didn't want a third party involved.

He couldn't take his eyes off Corrie as the waiter brought chocolate cheesecake for dessert and she smiled up at him asking for a refill of her coffee. He caught the waiter looking at the dangle on her necklace and then the V below it.

Sam quickly said, "I'll take a refill, too."

The waiter reluctantly gave his attention to Sam.

As Corrie took a bite of the cheesecake, smiled and slowly appreciated it, Sam had to shift in his chair. He'd never really thought about Corrie as a sensual woman but she was, and the way she was enjoying that cheesecake turned him on as fast as everything else about her tonight.

Maybe it was the holiday. Maybe it was the foil hearts hanging from the ceiling. Maybe it was Nathan and Sara sitting across from them looking so happy. Nathan couldn't keep his eyes off his wife and every once in a while, Sam saw him reach under the table and take her hand.

When the DJ began playing music, Corrie leaned close to Sam's shoulder. "I'm going to put a few requests in the basket. I'll be right back."

When Sam looked toward the wooden dais, he spied a small table with a wicker basket tied with a red bow. Beside it sat the sign—Drop In Requests. He realized he didn't even know what kind of music Corrie liked.

"Corrie looks beautiful tonight," Sara commented as if out of the blue.

Sam nodded. "Yes, she does."

"Is this a date?"

"Sara…" Nathan warned.

Sam waved his brother off. He and Sara had an understanding—straight talk between them. "It's sort of a date. We both needed a distraction and this seemed as good as anything."

"A distraction from what?" Nathan asked in that big brother tone.

Fortunately Sam didn't have to answer as Corrie returned to the table.

"What did you request?" he asked.

"Old standards. My mom was a connoisseur of fifties and sixties music. We listened to a lot of it together before she—" Corrie stopped and Sam knew she was thinking about those two years she took care of her mother.

"Elvis?" he asked.

"Yep, and doo-wop."

As the DJ began to play a slow ballad, Sam realized he could sit here and talk to Corrie, or they could do something interesting like dancing together. After all, this was a dance.

He stood and held out his hand to her. "Come on, let's see if we can match up our rhythms."

The words had more than one meaning and Corrie's cheeks flushed a bit. He smiled, settled his arm around her, and guided her to the dance floor. At first, Corrie seemed almost shy as Sam took her hand and wrapped his other arm around her. His palm kept wanting to land on that bare spot on her back.

Although the music was playing, the lack of conversation between them was obvious. Finally, Sam asked, "Did you enjoy dinner?"

"The food was great. So was the company. I've always liked Nathan, and Sara is wonderful—easy to talk to."

"Yes, she is. From the moment I met her, we had this honesty between us. We could say what we were thinking. She and Nathan came up to the cabin before Christmas to try and convince me to come home."

"Why didn't you? Why didn't you want to spend the holiday with the family?"

He could tell her why, but this didn't seem to be the right place or the right time. "I was researching foreign clinics and enjoying the silence. I hadn't had a vacation since Eric and I opened the practice. I needed the time away."

"I should mind my own business."

Corrie looked a little hurt and Sam didn't want her to be hurt. "No, that's not it. I don't want to think about then. I just want to think about now. I want to enjoy tonight… with you."

He tightened his hold on her just a little and now his hand did rest on that bare spot on her back. His thumb edged the circle. "You know, don't you, that this dress is provocative?"

"I couldn't really see the back when I tried it on. From the front it looked…sedate."

"Oh, yeah, with that slit up your thigh, it's really sedate."

Her eyes were all wide-eyed innocence as she asked, "Does that slit bother you?"

"Not any more than the hole in the back when you turn around."

She laughed and laid her cheek against his coat. He always thought of Corrie as independent, strong and capable. But tonight as he held her, she seemed fragile and delicate in his arms. She'd been through tough times. She'd taken care of her mother and postponed her future for that. Her discovery of her dad being unfaithful had been life-shattering. What that jerk in college had done to her had added to her outlook on relationships. No wonder she wanted to have a baby on her own. No strings, no one telling her what to do. With sole custody, she could make all of her own decisions. But that wasn't the way *he* wanted it. He'd never been passive. He'd never been just an onlooker. He reacted and got involved. If she had a baby, he'd be right there in that child's life.

He was so tempted to suggest this month when she ovulated that they just go to bed together and forget the hassle of the insemination. Yet he doubted if she'd agree to that. Part of Corrie wanted to remain detached. Getting involved personally wasn't part of the bargain.

Every time he breathed, he caught the scent of her perfume. As they swayed to the music, his thighs pressed into hers. The ambience of the most romantic day of the year floated around them, and he remembered the good part of having a woman in his life. He liked touching a woman's body. He liked matching wits. He liked the give-and-take of conversation, about serious subjects as well as trivial ones. Most of all, he liked a woman's softness against his hardness, the fitting together of parts that didn't make as much sense on their own.

Sam could feel Corrie's heart beating against his chest. She lifted her head and looked into his eyes.

He was aroused and the expression on her face told him she knew. His fingertips slid under the material of her dress on her back and he could feel the slight tremor that ran through her.

"Sam," she whispered.

"What?" He almost brushed her cheek as he lowered his head.

"What are we doing?"

"We're dancing."

"I feel as though we're doing something more than dancing."

"We're becoming friends, Corrie. Real friends."

"I don't think friends dance quite like this."

He couldn't tell if she was protesting or just analyzing what was happening. She wasn't pulling away. She wasn't saying they shouldn't be doing this and neither was he.

Now and then, another couple brushed by them. They didn't seem to care. One song melted into the next and they didn't break apart.

The need to kiss Corrie was building inside of Sam with each step they took, with each brush of his finger across her back, with each meeting of their gazes. He was enjoying the anticipation and the excitement as much as she was. When his lips brushed the lobe of her ear, he heard her small sigh. His jaw rubbed gently against her cheek and her hand tightened on his shoulder. Finally, when he thought they'd both waited long enough, he took a small soft kiss—not parting her lips, not invading her mouth, just a tantalizing temptation that they might want to take further.

Yes, kissing her could complicate their…partnership, but if they had an understanding—

Corrie's gaze focused on his, then slid over his shoulder. She went stiff in his arms.

"What's wrong?" he asked.

Before he could respond, he heard a voice from his past behind him.

Alicia Walker asked politely, as well as a bit seductively, "Do you mind if I cut in?"

Corrie's face told Sam the camaraderie they shared, the intimacy they'd dabbled in had just about evaporated into the perfumed air. As Corrie stepped away from him, Sam turned to face his ex-fiancée. Acid suddenly burned in his stomach, all the pleasure of the night forgotten.

Chapter Eight

What could Corrie do?

Alicia stood there, her hair upswept, her red dress perfect for her figure, her crystal necklace sparkling under the lights as brightly as her eyes. That sparkle was all for Sam and Corrie knew it.

She had no hold on Sam, no right to say, *He's mine. This is my dance. Go away.* Though that was exactly what she wanted to do.

Corrie stepped away from Sam and gave him what she hoped was a good reproduction of a smile. "See you back at the table," she said lightly. Truthfully, she didn't know what was going to happen after this dance with his ex-fiancée.

The expression on Sam's face gave nothing away, yet Corrie could see the small nerve at his jaw working. She didn't know if that was because he was glad to see Alicia or he wasn't.

Back at the table, Sara was frowning and Corrie knew she'd seen the whole thing, including Sam's kiss.

Nathan took one look at the two women, stood, leaned down and gave his wife a kiss. "You two talk. I'll be back when the dust clears."

Sara pushed her silky blond hair away from her face. "My husband's a wise man." She reached across to Corrie and patted her hand. "Also an understanding one. Are you upset?"

Corrie never confided in anyone easily, but Sara was so easy to talk to and seemed genuinely concerned.

"I think Sam and I are really starting to connect," she confided to Sara. "Alicia…interrupted that."

"Do you know her?" Sara asked.

"I'm acquainted with her. When she and Sam were engaged, she often came to the clinic. I saw her this afternoon at the hair salon and she said she might stop by the clinic again one of these days. I don't know if she found out Sam was going to be here tonight, or this is a coincidence."

"From what I've heard, I doubt if anything's a coincidence with Alicia Walker," Sara murmured, frowning.

Because she was usually upbeat, Sara's tone surprised Corrie. "I don't know what happened between them," Corrie admitted.

"Have you asked Sam?"

"He doesn't seem to want to talk about it. Do you know who broke off the engagement?"

Sara looked really torn and worried her bottom lip for a few seconds before her gaze unwaveringly met Corrie's. "I know, but I don't feel free to say. Sam has to tell you."

After studying Corrie for a few more moments, Sara asked, "You want more from Sam than for him to help you have a baby, don't you?"

Corrie was surprised for a moment that Sara knew, then realized she shouldn't be. Sam had told Nathan and Nathan apparently didn't keep secrets from his wife. This time she didn't think twice about telling Sara the truth. "I've been attracted to Sam for a while. I think he's a great guy. That's why I asked him to be a donor. The trouble is— I don't think men can be faithful. Even if a man says he can and he will, if another woman comes along and steps into any kind of gap that's developed in the relationship, he'll be gone."

Sara didn't jump in and try to convince Corrie otherwise as Corrie thought she might. Instead she asked, "Have you ever had a loyal friend who stood by you through thick and thin, no matter what? Who put you before their own concerns?"

Corrie thought about it. "My closest friend was my mother. After my parents divorced, I pulled away from everyone. If it hadn't been for her, I don't think I'd have known the kind of friendship you're talking about."

"Men and women are different, I'll grant you that," Sara said. "But the bottom line is—if someone has learned how to be loyal, whether they're male or female, they will be. Loyalty has a lot to do with fidelity. If you believe someone can be loyal, then you can believe in fidelity, can't you?"

"I suppose I never thought of those two things as the same before."

"Honestly, I don't know Ben very well. He's hard to get to know. But Sam and Nathan—" Sara tilted her head. "I think their dad taught his sons about basic values, how important they are, how to live by them. Nathan was so deeply in love with his first wife, Colleen, he didn't think he could ever let go of her. *I* thought he'd never let go. I left Rapid Creek to go back to Minneapolis thinking all I would ever have would be visits with Kyle and, I hoped, a friendship with Nathan. Then, when I left, he realized if he wanted love in his life again, he had to reach out and grab it. That meant grabbing me. His love for Colleen almost tore us apart, but it also showed me how deeply he can love. I don't believe fidelity would ever be an issue between us, and honestly, I think the same thing in true for Sam. He's one of the good guys, Corrie."

Corrie glanced over her shoulder, unable to help herself and then was sorry she did. Sam was holding Alicia in the same way he'd been holding *her*. His ex-fiancée was cuddled up against him and Corrie didn't know if that was Sam's doing or hers. They were talking as well as dancing and Corrie wondered what it was all about. Why had they broken up? Was there a way to fix what had happened?

Corrie turned to Sara. "They could get back together."

"I don't think that will happen, but you need to talk to Sam about it."

If she talked to Sam about it, she might not like what he had to say. But she might as well find out the truth now.

At the end of the song—something about fools falling in love—Corrie tried to keep her expression bland as she waited for Sam to come back to the table. Her back was to the dance floor but Sara's wasn't.

Sara said, "They've separated. I can't tell anything. They look amicable enough. Alicia's going to the ladies' room and she's smiling."

Sara's play-by-play told Corrie that Alicia had accomplished what she'd intended. Yet Corrie wasn't sure what that was. Making contact again? Stirring up old feelings?

A few minutes later when Sam returned to the table, he looked…different. The laugh lines around his eyes and mouth just made his face look drawn now as if he was wrestling with something.

Sara tried to awaken conversation. "So, when are you going skiing again?"

Sam looked as if he'd been lost in another world. "Sorry. What did you say?"

"Skiing. When are you going again? I really would like to learn and all of us could take a trek." Sara glanced at Corrie. "You're invited, too, of course."

"I don't know when I'll get out again," Sam said with a shrug. "Eric's taking some time off. We'll just have to wait and see."

Sam hadn't looked directly at Corrie once since he'd sat down and she was beginning to feel a remoteness emanating from him that hadn't been there before.

Testing the waters, she responded, "I told Eric I'd help you care for the animals when he's gone. He seemed to think that would be a good idea."

"If we don't have many surgery patients or boarders, that won't be necessary. I can handle it myself."

Tears threatened to pool in Corrie's eyes and she was determined not to let that happen. Her heart was weeping now and she knew why. Out on that dance floor, she and Sam had connected in more than one way. Body against body, they'd sizzled. He'd looked at her as if she were a desirable woman and she'd felt like one.

But now Alicia Walker had stepped back into his arms and everything had changed.

Only fools fall in love? She really should have learned that lesson before now.

Valentine's Day or not, floaty foil hearts dangling from the ceiling or not, the night had taken a decidedly different turn.

In the car on the way home, Sam rallied a bit. "If Nathan and I take Sara cross-country skiing, do you want to come along?"

"That depends. Do you want me to?"

He shot her a quick glance. "Sure. You strike me as the type who would really enjoy it. I don't know about Sara."

"Because she's a lawyer from the city?"

"I guess."

"I'm from the city, too."

"You're different from Sara."

"Not as refined?" She kept her voice simply questioning but Sam shot her another look.

"I don't think *refined* is the word. Before Sara met Nathan she had a sole focus and that was her career."

"And I let myself get diverted from mine."

"That wasn't a criticism, Corrie. In some ways I just see you as more adventurous than Sara."

Adventurous. She supposed that could be a good thing. "Sara and I have a lot in common. She told me she donated her eggs to Nathan and Colleen to get the money to save her mother's life. I quit school hoping that would prolong my mom's life."

Sam pulled up in front of her apartment. "I guess you're right. You're more alike than different. That old saying—you can't judge a book by its cover—holds true."

Tonight, Corrie had thought she'd changed her cover,

but apparently, looking more glamorous and seductive on the outside hadn't captured Sam's attention for very long...not when another woman could upset his evening the way Alicia had.

When Sam switched off the ignition, Corrie insisted, "You don't have to see me in."

Sam's jaw tightened. "I'll walk you to the door."

When he used that firm voice, she knew better than to argue with him.

As they reached the door, Jasper started barking from the other side.

"He'll have himself worked up into a frenzy if you don't open it."

The way Sam had acted, Corrie thought he'd say a quick good-bye and that would be it. But if he came in— She would ask him a few of the candid questions that were rolling around in her head.

After she unlocked the door, she pushed it open and Jasper danced all around her legs. She crouched down, petted him, cooed a few "I love you, too's" then rose to her feet.

Sam remarked, "If you need to take him out, go ahead."

"What I need are some answers, Sam."

He didn't give her a surprised, what-are-you-talking-about look. He just shoved his hands into his trouser pockets. "What kind of answers?"

Jasper sniffed around Sam's shoes, then trotted over to the sofa, jumped up and settled in the corner.

"We were having a good time tonight, at least I was. Then suddenly Alicia Walker's there and you turn into a different person."

His expression was troubled. "I didn't mean for that to happen."

"Whether you meant it or not, it did, and I felt as if you didn't want me there anymore."

"Corrie, that's not it at all!"

"Are you still in love with her?"

"No."

His answer was quick, but Corrie wondered if it had come too fast. "That's what it looks like. From where I was sitting, you seemed upset and maybe that's because you still want to be with her."

"I can never be with Alicia again. I can never trust her."

There was such pain in Sam's eyes that Corrie suggested, "Why don't we sit?"

He raked his fingers through his hair. "This isn't something I want to talk about."

"Maybe you don't want to, but maybe you should. If Alicia upsets you that strongly—"

"It's not Alicia. It's what she did."

Reluctantly he crossed to the sofa and sat beside the dog. Absently, he settled his big gentle hand on the dog's head, then leaned against the back cushion. He was definitely wrestling with something that had happened between him and Alicia, and Corrie wanted to know what that was.

Perching on the sofa beside him, she asked, "Who broke it off?"

He looked straight ahead. "I did."

"Was she unfaithful?"

"I could have handled *that* a lot better. Not that we'd still be together if she had been."

"What happened?" Corrie prompted gently.

Pulling open his tie, he swung his attention back to Corrie. "She had an abortion and didn't tell me."

A small gasp escaped Corrie's lips. "Oh, Sam! I'm sorry."

"She didn't even tell me she was pregnant. One day when I got home there was a call on the answering machine from her doctor to make a follow-up appointment. I knew it was her gynecologist and I wanted to know what kind of follow-up it was. When I confronted her, she told me."

"She didn't want children?"

"There are a few ways to look at this—she didn't want children, she didn't want *my* children or she didn't want a child *now.*"

"But you were engaged. Had you talked about it?"

"We'd talked about it, but apparently I hadn't listened well enough. I heard what I wanted to hear. When I brought it up she'd say, 'We'll discuss it again after we're married' or she'd tell me we needed a few years to ourselves first before we considered having kids. That seemed plausible and reasonable, but I should have been more perceptive. I should have explored *why* she didn't want to have kids right away. Maybe then I would have found out she didn't know if she wanted to have them *at all.*"

No wonder Sam had taken the opportunity to be her sperm donor. He wanted to be a dad and he saw this as a way to do it. "Did Alicia know you were going to be there tonight?"

"She's friends with one of the members on the planning committee. He had a list of the people who'd bought tickets. She didn't even try to hide the fact she came on purpose to see me."

Corrie guessed where that was going to lead. Alicia

wanted to get back together with Sam. "Did you talk about what happened?"

"No. We made polite conversation. I didn't want to get into anything on the dance floor. I didn't want to get into anything...period. I think she sensed that."

Corrie understood about not wanting to confront the pain that hurt worst. That's why she avoided deep conversation with her dad. Would Sam ever get over what Alicia had done? The sense of betrayal?

Corrie and Sam were a real pair. Each of them wanted a child, but they each wanted a child independently of having a partner. Trust was a giant issue that could be a stumbling block, even to having a close friendship.

Sam took Corrie's hand. "I'm sorry tonight blew up in my face. It wasn't fair to you. I was having a good time, a great time, and I shouldn't have let Alicia interfere with that."

"I can see why she did. What happened between you isn't something you can just slough off."

"When you asked me to be a sperm donor, I had to really think about it. I didn't want to do it just to salve my ego. It really was an honor—the fact that you considered me good father material. But that's not why I said yes. I said yes because I want to be a dad even if it's not in the usual sense."

Jasper lifted his head, stretched and hopped down off the sofa. He trotted over to a corner table where his leash lay.

"I'd better take him out."

"And I'd better go."

When Sam stood, so did she. They were toe to toe, close enough that she could smell his cologne, close enough that if he leaned forward, he could kiss her.

But he didn't. Instead, he said, "No one knows what

happened with Alicia except for my family. I'd like to keep it that way."

"Of course."

After a long look into her eyes, he gave a short nod. She walked him to the door.

On the stoop, he reached out and touched her cheek. "Happy Valentine's Day, Corrie."

His words were sincere and, as Sam turned and walked away, she knew she'd irrevocably lost her heart to him.

"You want to tell me why Corrie has ignored you all week?" Eric asked the following Friday, as he took his stethoscope from around his neck and poked it into his pocket.

Sam was tempted to deny Eric's conclusion, but he didn't because it was true. When he walked into an exam room, Corrie didn't stay any longer than necessary. She did what was required of her and left. She didn't come in early. She didn't hang around after hours. Both were unusual for her.

He knew what was at the bottom of it, but didn't know what to do about it. "She thinks I still love Alicia."

"I heard what happened at the Valentine's Day dance. Alicia was never shy. That was one reason you liked her."

The benefit or curse of a small town was that everyone knew everyone else's business. No, Alicia hadn't been shy about anything. Coy, maybe, but not shy. Now he wondered why that quality had been attractive. Now he simply saw it as part of her selfish attitude. She went after what she wanted no matter what the cost.

"I also heard you and Corrie were getting along quite nicely before Alicia cut in." Eric's smile was sly.

"Heard from whom?" Sam asked, angrily.

"I'm not going to say. So it's true, huh?"

Eric was enjoying this just a little too much. "I'm attracted to Corrie. I'll admit that."

"And you're trying to make a baby with her. One and one isn't adding up to two. Why use artificial means?"

Hadn't Sam entertained that same thought? "Because I'm not interested in another relationship. And Corrie? Well, she has trust issues, too. It just wouldn't be a good idea."

Sitting on the corner of the receptionist's desk, Eric proclaimed, "I know just what you need."

"I'm afraid to ask."

"You need to come with me tonight to the Tavern."

Patches was wagging his tail against Sam's leg, and Sam reached down to scratch his ears. "I don't think so."

"This is exactly the problem, Sam. You spend your life with your dog. I understand you don't want to get involved with a woman. So don't. Come out with me tonight, dance, drink. Who knows? Maybe you'll get lucky. No relationship. Just some fun."

Since his divorce, Eric had dated woman after woman. Pretty soon, the eligible women in Rapid Creek would be exhausted and he'd have to move on to the next nearest town. That chasing-capturing-chasing-again pattern just didn't appeal to Sam.

The back door to the clinic suddenly opened and Corrie came rushing in. When she saw them, she stopped. "Oh, hi. Sorry. I didn't mean to interrupt."

"You're not interrupting," Eric assured her. "I'm just trying to convince Sam to come to the Tavern tonight to have some fun. Do you want to come along?"

"Uh, no. That's okay. I just came back for some of

that special food for Jasper. You know, the one with all the vitamins."

Eric rolled his eyes. "Two people who live for their dogs." He stood. "As soon as I hang up my lab coat, I'm out of here. Sam, if you change your mind, meet me there. I'll be there most of the evening watching the big-screen TV. The same goes for you, Corrie. A little excitement in your life wouldn't hurt one bit."

After Eric left Corrie with Sam, she avoided his gaze. Crossing to the shelf on one side of the reception area, she picked up a few cans of the dog food she'd mentioned.

"See ya," Eric called from the hall.

After both Sam and Corrie called good-bye and the back door closed, Sam asked Corrie, "Did you really come back in here for dog food?"

She glanced at him over her shoulder. "Why else would I have come back?"

"Maybe to talk to me. You haven't said two words all week."

"You're exaggerating."

"Not by much."

"Maybe I don't know what to say to you, Sam. Did you ever think of that?"

"You never had any trouble talking about the weather before," he quipped, the honesty he usually appreciated in Corrie now making him uncomfortable.

"We've gone beyond the weather," she insisted quietly. "Last Saturday night we were acting as if we were on a date. Then suddenly Alicia waltzes back into your life and you're thrown for a loop. Maybe I haven't talked to you all week because there's a question I need to ask you. Do you still want to go through with the artificial insemination?"

He could see she was upset and trying not to show it. She was afraid he wouldn't go through with their plans. Sam knew their second attempt would probably happen in the next week or so. He'd been thinking about it for the past few days.

Slowly, he crossed to Corrie. His hand on her shoulder, he nudged her to face him and looked into her very pretty blue eyes. "Nothing momentous happened Saturday night."

"You should have seen your face when Alicia cut in."

"What did you see?" he asked gently.

"I'm not sure, but something about you changed."

"I got slapped in the face by what had happened between us. I relived all over again the moment when she told me she'd had an abortion."

It was obvious that Corrie believed he still loved Alicia. He knew he didn't. This was all about the child he'd lost, not the woman he'd lost, but he could say that until he was blue in the face and he still didn't know if Corrie would believe him.

"As far as I'm concerned, nothing has changed," he assured her. "I want my life to move forward. Part of that process is helping you get pregnant. If that happens, I'll become a dad. Nothing would make me happier."

She studied him for a very long time and then let out a pent-up breath. "I believe you."

To his chagrin, Sam realized he wanted to seal their renewed bargain with something other than a handshake. He wanted to kiss Corrie Edwards until her teeth rattled. He wanted to sink his hands into that curly hair and just stay there for a while. But he didn't do either.

Instead, he took a step back and asked, "Would you

like to go to the Tavern tonight? We could get in a few dances and make up for Valentine's Day."

"No, I can't," Corrie said quickly. "I have some other things I really have to do."

Sam guessed that wasn't true. Corrie was determined she wasn't going to get hurt. All she wanted was a baby.

All *he* wanted was to be a dad.

Then why was he so disappointed she'd said no?

Chapter Nine

"The doctor is delayed," the smiling nurse said to Sam and Corrie as they sat waiting at the hospital. "She had two deliveries this morning, but she'll be here shortly and then we can get started."

As the nurse left the waiting room, Corrie glanced at Sam. She'd called him at 7:00 a.m. this morning, after she'd phoned her doctor to say that she was ovulating again. This week the tension hadn't been quite as bad between them since their talk on Friday. She'd tried not to ignore him, which wasn't hard because she couldn't. But she kept her distance, because when he touched her, or she touched him, the world always tilted.

He had the power to completely disrupt her life and that was the last thing she wanted. No matter what he said, she felt he still had ties to Alicia Walker, or at least unresolved feelings for her. They weren't finished yet. She wished they were but then she'd made lots of wishes in her life that hadn't come true. Letting go of a love gone wrong took time. She knew that from personal experience. Sam had been ready to *marry* Alicia. That hurt wouldn't go away for a while.

Unlike Alicia, Corrie didn't want to keep secrets from Sam. She hadn't yet told him about the lawyer's job offer and she felt she really should. Maybe now was the best time. They were the only ones in the waiting room.

"Shirley Klinedinst's lawyer, Colin Bancroft, came to see me."

When Sam shifted toward her, his arm lodged against hers. "He found a home for Jasper?"

"Not exactly. I mean, he wants me to take Jasper. Apparently the first couple of weeks were a test."

"To see if he'd be happy with you?"

"Not just that. He made me a job offer."

Sam frowned. "What kind of job offer?"

Corrie liked being near Sam like this…talking, touching, sharing their lives. In a gray cable-knit sweater and black jeans, he was as sexy as ever today. Pulling her attention away from that train of thought, she explained, "Apparently Shirley wasn't exactly what she seemed. She and her husband had lots of money even though no one ever knew it. She wants her house and the grounds to be turned into a shelter for homeless animals and she'd like me to run it. The salary's amazing. If I don't want to actually live there and take care of the animals, I have the choice of directing the facility—hiring employees, writing up the budget, running the whole organization. It would pay the same."

"You can't seriously be thinking about accepting the offer."

Sam's tone surprised her. "Why not?"

"If you have a baby, you can't run something like that."

"Of course, I can."

"It would be a consuming job, Corrie, especially if you did the hands-on work. Clinic hours are tough enough. This would be day and night. You can't be a mother and take that on, too."

She moved and they were no longer physically connected. "Wait a minute. I thought you were a man of the new millennium. What you're suggesting is old-fashioned prejudice."

"No, it's not. It's experience talking. My mother left us to pursue a career. I know all about women who have goals other than their family."

"You believe a woman can have a family and that's all she can do? Really, Sam, I'm going to be a single mom. I can make ends meet on the salary your clinic pays me, but with this job, I could do a lot more."

"What about your time?" Sam protested. "A child needs time—lots of it. Quality time is important, but quantity is, too. What would you do, hire a nanny to take care of the baby while you're formulating a budget, hiring help and seeing to animals' care?"

The truth was, she hadn't thought that far ahead. "I'm not even pregnant yet, Sam. I might not *get* pregnant. I have to consider this."

Sam's eyes narrowed. "When did Shirley's lawyer make you this offer?"

"A week and a half ago."

His frown was backed up by the frustration in his eyes. "And you're just telling me now?"

Why did she feel so defensive? This was *her* concern

and *her* decision to make. "I wanted to consider the offer first. I have, and I like the idea of running a shelter for animals. I'd feel I was making a difference and doing something worthwhile."

"What about going back to school?"

"I can do that eventually. With this salary I could save money for tuition quickly."

"I still have to wonder where a baby fits into all of this." His gaze held hers and wouldn't let her turn away.

"Of course if I get pregnant, that child will be my primary focus. But having a baby doesn't eliminate other aspirations."

Sam didn't look convinced. "How long do you have to make the decision?"

"I have until April first. If I don't want to do any of it, I still keep Jasper, will receive a stipend for taking care of him and a developer will buy Shirley's property. The rest of the money will be given to the Humane Society."

A nurse came hurrying into the waiting room. "The doctor's ready for you now."

Sam looked at Corrie as if to ask, *Are you sure you want to go through with this?* But she *was* sure.

"I'm ready," she told Sam and the nurse.

As she walked to the room where she'd undergo the second insemination procedure, she was determined to take control of her life. She wouldn't jump into this job offer impulsively, but she would consider it seriously and do whatever was best for her, no matter what Sam thought.

Corrie unlocked the door to the clinic Saturday evening and knocked the snow from her boots before she stepped inside. Snow had been falling since late afternoon. Eric had taken off yesterday for parts unknown. Last night, Sam had checked on the animals. Tonight she was doing it.

She'd no sooner turned on the lights in the reception area when she heard the back door open.

She unzipped her parka, slid it off and threw it over a wooden bench. She was halfway to the kennel when Sam appeared. His boots were caked with snow and snow-flakes nestled in his hair.

"What are you doing here?" she asked him. "It's my turn to check on the animals."

Ever since their second insemination attempt on Wed-nesday, they'd both been on edge. The conversation they'd had at the hospital hadn't helped. She didn't like friction between them, either on a personal level or a pro-fessional level.

Still she couldn't help but ask, "Are you checking up on me?" He never had before, but there was a first time for everything, she supposed.

"No, I'm not checking up on you. I didn't want you to shovel the walk. We've already got about five inches out there. I thought I'd take the snowblower over it. The plow will be here in the morning for the parking lot."

As Sam came inside, he took off his gloves and stuffed them into his pockets. Dressed in a black parka with a hood and black boots, he looked bigger, broader and even more virile than usual.

"I can make a pot of coffee while you're outside. It will warm you up when you come in."

"Coffee sounds good. I'll be back in about fifteen minutes."

When Sam returned from clearing the walk, Corrie had finished with the dogs in the kennel and was washing up.

"Coffee's ready," she called to him, quickly drying her hands and joining him in the small lounge. He'd already poured her a mug.

"Milk and sugar, right?" he asked.

She knew he liked his black. "Right."

The silent clinic seemed to press in on them as they both took seats on the love seat, mugs of coffee in hand. He took a sip of coffee and set his mug on the table beside the love seat. His navy sweatshirt had seen many washings. His jeans were worn. But he'd never looked more attractive to her and she'd never been more attracted to him. Her hand was trembling a little so she set her mug on the table beside her, too.

"I thought you might have plans for tonight," she ventured.

"By that, you mean plans with Alicia? I told you, Corrie, I don't intend to get involved with her again."

"But do you still have feelings for her?"

"No. I have regrets. I wish I had been more clearheaded about her before we'd gotten engaged. Whatever happened, it's over. Now I'm looking for something different in my life. Maybe the same thing you're looking for."

"Parenthood?"

"Yes. Have you given any more thought to Bancroft's job offer?"

"I'm waiting for a decision to feel right. I'm waiting to find out—"

"If you're pregnant."

"Yes. Because if I'm not, we only have one more try. That's all I can afford."

"I told you I'm paying half. That should make your money go twice as far. Besides..." He appraised her for a very long time. "If you really want a baby, and you want to keep trying, there *is* a natural way to do it."

Was he suggesting what she thought he was suggesting?

He shifted toward her and covered her hand with his. "We had something going on Valentine's Day. I know you felt it."

She'd felt it all right…in every fiber of her being. Just like she felt it now with his palm on her fingers. Heat…electricity…awareness so strong she couldn't turn away. When his body had been pressed against hers, nothing in the world had mattered more than being right there with him.

His thumb stroked over the top of her hand. "I finally thought you were letting your guard down a little."

His caress melted away any reserve she had left. "I've had years of practice keeping it up."

"For one moment, just one moment, can you try to believe you don't have a past or a future?" he asked, his voice husky. "Can you just think about right now?"

Could she believe in that fantasy? Even for just a little while? The even bigger question was, did she want to?

But gazing into Sam's intensely dark-brown eyes, remembering his kisses, desiring him in a way she'd never desired another man, Corrie felt living in the present just might be possible.

Sam's arm slowly went around her, and she didn't resist the thrill of being close to him again. Lately when she was around Sam, she felt so good. He seemed to appreciate her, respect her and even at times admire her. He listened when she spoke to him as if she had something important to say. The result of all that was simple—she was even more attracted to him.

As his hand slid under her hair, she expected a fast, tempestuous kiss. Instead, he leaned his cheek against hers and simply let them both feel the sensation of skin on skin, mouths close, breaths almost commingling. Flames of temptation leapt around them whenever they were within two feet of each other. Now they became a full-blown fire. Corrie wanted Sam's lips on hers. She needed Sam's lips on hers. With a little moan, she tilted her head and that was the only signal Sam needed.

Sam's lips took hers seductively, erotically, as if he'd been waiting much too long to kiss her again. She knew the feeling. She tried to absorb every little sensation—the warmth of his lips, the firmness of them, the way he pressed and convinced and coaxed until his tongue was in her mouth and she was stroking him, lost and loving every minute of what was happening between them. One of his hands cupped the back of her head as the other drifted down her neck, over her sweater, and paused over her breast.

Although Corrie had had sex with one man a long time ago, she hadn't forgotten it. She'd felt awkward. He'd seemed to grope at her. So any fantasy she'd envisioned had burst like the proverbial bubble. She'd never fallen for the hype about sex on the covers of magazines, had never expected a better experience than the one she'd had. But here with Sam, fantasies came alive again. Their kiss was so much more than she'd ever anticipated a kiss could be. It made her want. It made her burn. It made her believe again that maybe two bodies could come together as one. Sam's touch was so light at first, so gently persuasive, she didn't recognize it for the teasing that it was.

His tongue explored her mouth. She tried to push her

breast into his palm, wanting more contact, needing his touch as much as she needed air to breathe.

"Slow down," he whispered against her lips. "We don't have to rush."

Maybe not, but she was afraid if they didn't, everything would disappear—the feelings, the excitement, the living in the moment. So instead of trying to increase her pleasure, she decided to give him pleasure.

She found the edge of his sweatshirt and her fingers tunneled under it. When her skin met his, he groaned and broke the kiss. "You're not playing fair."

"I'm not playing," she assured him, and let her hand trail up his chest until her fingers laced in his chest hair.

He bowed his head onto her shoulder and kissed her neck, kissed behind her ear and took her earlobe into his mouth and sucked on it.

"Sam," she gasped.

"I'm not playing, either."

This was serious. And if it was serious—

Her thoughts evaporated as Sam's lips kissed down the V-neck of her sweater. "You have freckles here," he noticed, glancing up at her with a smile. "They weren't there the night you wore the black dress."

"I covered them with makeup," she admitted.

"Your freckles are sexy." He kissed one for emphasis.

"The boys in high school didn't think so."

"They were too young to know any better. I'm mature enough to appreciate every one of them. In fact, now I'm wondering where else you might have freckles."

She felt her cheeks growing hot but she bantered back anyway. "I used to sunbathe in a bikini so I have freckles lots of places."

"You're killing me here, Corrie."

No, she wasn't. She was turning him on. She liked the feeling so much that she wanted to do more of it. Arousing Sam Barclay gave her a feeling of power... power that she'd never possessed before.

He kissed her again. This time her fingers passed down his chest and edged his belt buckle.

Maybe Sam hadn't wanted to hurry before, but now she could feel his urgency as well as her own. They were heading someplace she'd never been and she couldn't wait to get there.

"Do you mind if I take off your sweater?" he murmured in her ear.

"I don't mind...if I can take off your sweatshirt."

When he laughed, she reached for the hem of his shirt. He lifted her sweater and their arms got tangled. They laughed again, freely, enjoying the moment, enjoying each other. As Sam kissed her, he unfastened her bra and then cupped her breasts in his palms. Though she didn't want to be, she was embarrassed and couldn't meet his gaze. He wouldn't let her get away with that. "Look at me, Corrie."

She lifted her head and the desire she saw in his eyes gave her renewed courage. "Don't stop," she murmured as his thumbs rounded her nipples.

"I'll have to stop eventually or we can't get to the next part." She saw the amusement in his eyes and knew he wasn't laughing at her, but rather enjoying her.

"The next part?" she joked. "I wonder if that goes something like this." Her hand cupped him and the smile left his face.

"You've just raised the stakes."

"I'm ready if you are."

"More than ready," he muttered, unsnapping his jeans and then unfastening the zipper. When he lowered his fly, his erection pressed against his briefs. Her shyness fled as she thought about touching him, seeing him, feeling him inside of her. She hadn't experienced an orgasm all those years ago. Could she with Sam? Would she?

As if he didn't want to give her too much time to think, he stooped down, unzipped one of her boots and then the other. The next minute, he was pulling her jeans and panties down over her hips and she was kicking them off onto the floor. After he pulled off his boots, he slid out of his jeans and briefs.

Corrie was in awe of his body. He was absolutely beautifully made. His arms were muscled, his chest thickly matted with dark hair, his stomach taut. As her eyes arrowed below his navel, she felt all quivery inside.

He took her hand and drew her down to the braided rug.

She lay back, enjoying the excitement and anticipation, impatient for Sam's body on top of hers. But she soon found out Sam still wasn't going to rush. His kisses were long and wet and deep. His hands brushed in sensual strokes over her breasts, down her stomach, between her legs. She trembled and he noticed.

"This is going to feel so good, Corrie. I promise you."

Did Sam keep his promises? That question turned into pure sensation as his fingers slid inside her and she became wet and hot and ready.

"Now, Sam. I want you *now*."

"Raise your knees," he suggested.

When she did, he pushed inside of her…slowly…oh, so slowly. As he filled her, tears burned in her eyes. Her emotions were so close to the surface, she was afraid he'd see them all.

But he closed his eyes as he thrust into her, building their pleasure. She held on to him, clutching his shoulders, her skin becoming as slick as his.

To Corrie's surprise, Sam went perfectly still.

"Am I doing something wrong?" she asked, worried that this might be the first time happening all over again.

"You're doing everything right. I'm just letting us enjoy the moment."

"When I feel as if I'm going to topple off the edge of the world?"

"We'll topple off together. Synchronicity."

"Maybe I can't, Sam. Maybe—"

"Relax, Corrie, and just go with it. Go with me."

He began moving in and out, slowly at first, then faster. She got caught up in the rhythm and was breathing as hard as he was and rocking just as fast.

When her nails raked his back, he muttered, "I knew there was a tigress in there somewhere."

She felt wild and free and sexual, ready to be somebody new. Her climax came so suddenly her world burst apart before she was ready. One moment she was hanging on to Sam as he took their pleasure to a height she had never imagined, the next, colors were bursting all around her, her body tensing as tingly fire danced on every nerve ending.

When she gasped his name, Sam found his release, too. He shuddered, held her tight then collapsed onto her, his cheek against hers.

"Am I crushing you?" Sam asked, not moving an inch.

Corrie liked the feel of his weight on her, liked his legs

tangled with hers, liked his face within kissing distance. "No, she murmured, unable to put all that into words.

Nevertheless, a few moments later, he raised himself up on his elbows. She fell halfway to earth fast. The concern in his brown eyes brought her the rest of the way.

"What are you thinking?" he asked.

"I'm thinking we just complicated everything."

"Can't friends have sex?"

"And remain friends?" She shook her head. "I don't know, Sam. I really don't know."

"We can just think of sex between us as a means to an end. If you don't get pregnant through the artificial insemination, you can get pregnant this way. We'll have unlimited opportunities for it to happen."

No, what they would have were unlimited opportunities for him to break her heart. This might just be sex for Sam, but for her it was a whole lot more. If she did this again…

She couldn't do this again. She'd felt too much. She loved Sam Barclay and that was something she could never tell him. What if she *was* pregnant? What if they had to raise a child together?

Raise a child together? When had she started thinking in those terms? This was *her* child. She was going to make the decisions.

What child? Right now, all you have to deal with is not having sex with Sam again.

"Uh-oh, you're thinking. I can tell." He maneuvered himself up and onto the sofa and sat there unabashedly naked, just staring at her.

"This can't happen again, Sam. I mean it was great, but…I can't have sex with you as if it's a recreational activity."

"If it's a recreational activity, no one gets hurt," Sam maintained.

"I don't believe that's true. Sex by itself, just for sex's sake, isn't something I want to participate in. But sex between friends who care about each other, even a little bit, will become more than sex. We're asking for trouble. I don't want it."

Sam kept his gaze on hers for a long time. "Did you want this today?"

She knew how Sam thought. He was already wondering if he'd forced her into it somehow, persuaded her when she hadn't been altogether willing. And that wasn't the case.

"Yes, I wanted it."

"But you don't want it to happen again."

She did, with all her heart, but not because she desired Sam, not because she wanted to feel pleasure, not because sex was a need she wanted to fill, but because she loved him. He didn't love her. So it couldn't happen again.

"No, I don't," she lied.

Those three words seemed to galvanize him. He gathered his clothes and began dressing. Then, being Sam, he picked up her clothes and handed them to her so she could cover herself. After all, if she'd decided this wouldn't happen again, she might be embarrassed to be naked in front of him.

She reached out and grabbed his arm. "Sam, it really was good."

"Sure," he muttered, stepping into his briefs, and then his jeans. "I'll check on the dogs in the kennel, then I'll follow you home. The snow's getting deep. I want to make sure you get there safely."

He'd said that once before and she'd had an accident.

Sam couldn't prevent another accident from happening, but she could.

And she would. Parenting together could be difficult enough. As lovers, it would be impossible. She wanted to keep her independence, and she never wanted to be hurt like her mother. The lawyer's offer for her to be director of the homeless shelter was looking better and better.

If she took it, she wouldn't be under Sam's watchful eye. Her life would be her own.

Chapter Ten

Corrie rang Sam's doorbell Friday evening, her hands sweaty in her gloves, her heart fluttering so fast she was sure it was going to switch into overdrive. Since they'd made love almost a week ago, she'd felt all churned up. Now...

Sam opened the door and looked momentarily surprised. Then his face went blank.

There was no point in making small talk. "I just came from my doctor's. I'm pregnant." She couldn't keep the excitement from her voice or the smile from curving her lips. She wanted to hug him, kiss him, shout for joy, but she wasn't at all sure what his reaction was going to be.

However, he smiled back, took her hand and pulled her inside. "I can't believe it actually happened."

"Me, either, but it has. I'm so happy I could turn somersaults."

"I'd like to see that," he teased.

All of a sudden she felt embarrassed with him. He'd seen more of her than she'd ever shown anyone. She'd been more open with him than she'd ever been with a man. Neither of them had handled what happened between them very well. For the past week, they'd avoided being alone in the same room together.

He seemed to catch her mood and the amusement left his eyes. "When are you due?"

"My due date is November eleventh, We'll have a baby by Thanksgiving."

"Wouldn't that be a real gift?"

She could see he meant it. "The greatest blessing of all." Her throat grew tight and she coughed to cover up the surge of emotion that almost seemed to overwhelm her.

Sam held her by the shoulders. "I know how happy you are about this. It's okay to let yourself feel it."

It would be so easy to cuddle into Sam's arms, so wonderful to kiss him again and even let him lead her to bed to celebrate. But she couldn't do that for so many reasons. Alicia Walker was one very pointed reason. Sam was still on the rebound and no matter what he said, she'd seen his turmoil when he'd danced with the woman. A second was her own doubts about men and fidelity and their ability to love unconditionally. She'd never witnessed it firsthand. And now it loomed very large on the horizon with their baby, the custody issue and her desire to retain control over her life and her child's.

Pulling away from Sam, she opened her purse and extracted a list. "There are so many things I have to do."

"Like?" he prompted.

"I have to go to the pharmacy and buy vitamins. I'll have to stock up on baby supplies. I have a magazine with a list of everything I'll need for the layette."

"And you have to do all this tonight?" he asked with a grin.

"No, of course not, but I want to get started."

"Do you have to go home first?"

"Yes, and I really should bring Jasper along with me so he's not lonely."

Sam nodded to Patches who was asleep in his bed by the sofa. "Why don't I come with you? Jasper and Patches can stay in the van and keep each other company. We won't be in the store that long."

"You want to shop for baby things?" She knew how most men felt about shopping.

"Let's just say I could use an education in baby supplies." His gaze never left hers. "If I'm going to spend time around our baby, I'll have to know what I'll need and how to take care of him or her."

A panicked look must have crossed her face.

"I imagine I'll be babysitting some of the time," he continued.

"Babysitting?"

"Sure, or do you intend never to go out on your own again?"

He had a point there and she wasn't sure at all yet what she was going to do about working.

"You've got nine months to work this out, Corrie, and I'll help you."

The question was—would his help complicate her life or simplify it?

It would be fun to have somebody to share the joy with.

What harm would it do if Sam came along on a preliminary shopping trip with her?

"Do you want to go to Target?"

"I've never been in the baby section. This could be an eye-opener," Sam said.

They did as Sam suggested. After he followed Corrie to her place, they let the dogs run. Then they piled into Sam's van. The dogs seemed happy just to sit in the back together while Corrie and Sam left them and found their way to the baby section of the department store. Corrie was so happy, she was afraid to believe she really was pregnant. As they studied the baby bottles, the diapers and other necessary supplies, she turned to Sam. "I just can't believe it's true—that I'm really pregnant!"

"If your doctor says it's true, then it's true."

"Thank you, Sam."

"My part in this was minor," he said wryly.

"Without you, I wouldn't be pregnant. I just don't think I could have used a stranger's sperm."

Looking more serious than happy for her, he responded, "I think if you had used a stranger's sperm, this would have been easier for you, though. A stranger wouldn't care which bottles you bought, or which diapers or whether or not you worked after you had your baby."

Her heart sank. "Sam…"

"If you stay at the clinic, you can work part-time. You can take off whenever you need to."

"I need a full-time salary, Sam, not a part-time one. I have to think of the future, not just now."

"I'm thinking of the future, too, and how the time you

spend or don't spend with your baby is going to matter later." His jaw set and he seemed determined to make her think his way.

"Didn't you tell me your mother wasn't happy being a homemaker?" she probed. "Didn't you tell me that you and your brothers knew that? I believe the best way to take care of my child is for me to be happy, too."

"You're not happy at the clinic?"

"Oh, Sam. This isn't about whether I'm happy at the clinic or not. It's about a new opportunity to expand my world and my child's. You've got to give me time to come up with a plan that I think is best. You can't try to argue me into looking at your side and only your side. We'll have constant friction. Work certainly won't be a pleasure, and raising a child will become one confrontation after another. You don't want that, do you?"

"Of course I don't, but I also don't think you can abandon a child to a new job and think you're doing the best thing for the baby."

"My child will *never* be abandoned. You know what kind of relationship I had with my mother. Do you think for a minute I don't want the same kind for me and *my* daughter or son?"

Corrie could see that Sam's feelings about this were deeply rooted so she went on. "My mom worked part-time when I was young, but after the divorce, she had to work full-time. Don't you get it, Sam? It's a fact that women don't depend on men anymore. They don't *want* to depend on men."

Sam's eyes were the deepest brown Corrie had ever seen them, and he looked as if he was about to erupt. She felt close to the boiling-over stage herself.

Just then, she heard, "Sam! Corrie! What are you doing here?"

When Corrie glanced over her shoulder, she spotted Sara.

Sam was the first to recover. "What are *you* doing here?" he questioned his sister-in-law.

"Nathan and Kyle are making me a surprise," she said, making quote marks with her fingers. "I think it's a chocolate cake with peanut butter icing. They know that's my favorite. Kyle needed a refill on his inhaler so I decided to come get that."

"So what are you two doing here?" Sara asked.

"I'm pregnant," Corrie admitted quietly.

Sara gave her a big hug. "Congratulations."

"The second try at artificial insemination was a success." Corrie wanted to make that clear. She didn't want people to think she and Sam had slept together to make a baby, even though they *had* slept together.

"That's wonderful. Should I keep quiet about this, or can I tell Nathan and Galen?"

"You can tell them," Sam said with a shrug. "Everyone will know soon enough, when Corrie starts showing."

"That could be a few months," Sara offered. "As soon as you tell a few people, everyone will know. But the family can keep it quiet if that's what you want."

"I guess that will be up to Corrie."

"I just found out this evening and I'm trying to absorb it. Go ahead and tell Nathan and Galen. I'm sure Sam will want to tell Ben, too. But other than family, I think we'll keep it quiet for a while."

As if Sara sensed the tension between them, she tucked her pharmacy bag under her arm. "I'll let you two alone. I imagine you have a lot to discuss." After a hug for Sam and a final wave goodbye, Sara walked down the aisle and headed for the front of the store.

Corrie didn't break the uncomfortable silence.

Sam finally concluded, "We *do* have a lot to discuss, including what happened Sunday."

"When I went to your place tonight, I was so happy and excited, Sam. But now, you're making me wish I had gone to that fertility clinic in Minneapolis. I think our research trip is over for tonight. I'd like to go home."

Without waiting for Sam, she headed for the front of the store. He was not going to bully her or boss her or tell her what to do. She wouldn't let him, not now, and not after the baby was born.

The baby.

Their baby.

Sam's baby.

Corrie's heart hurt. Each day that passed, it hurt a little more. Sam had backed off. In the past five days, he hadn't spoken to her about the job…or about their baby. Was he giving her time to think, or was he giving himself time to build a persuasive argument that would convince her he was right?

By Wednesday morning when Corrie exited an exam room after another professional—and *only* professional—consultation with Sam, her turmoil was giving her a headache. Not only were her feelings for Sam interfering with her usually calm life, but her dad was coming on Sunday and staying for a week!

When Corrie spotted Alicia standing by the receptionist's counter, the pounding in her head increased. Her first thought was to go up to the woman and tell her Sam wasn't here. But that would be stupid. Corrie had absolutely no say whatsoever in Sam's life.

She wanted it that way, didn't she?

The truth was, she didn't know what she wanted where Sam was concerned. They were two reasonable adults for goodness sakes! Why was everything getting so muddled?

Alicia spotted Corrie. Giving her one of those fake smiles, she beckoned to her.

Corrie crossed to her.

"Jenny was just telling me she didn't know how long Sam would be with his patient. Do you have any idea? I'd really like to see him for a few minutes."

"He'll be finished shortly. He's just giving final instructions."

Jenny interjected, "I told Miss Walker that he doesn't have a break between patients."

"I only need to talk to him for about two minutes, just to make a lunch or supper date. I promise, I won't hold him up. I know how busy he is," Alicia said sweetly.

Jenny gave Corrie a what-can-we-do look, and Corrie knew this was Sam's business, not theirs.

The door to the exam room opened and Sam came striding out. When he saw the three women at the desk, he stopped. The decision of whether he wanted to talk to his ex-fiancée was his; Corrie was just afraid that he did.

"Alicia," he greeted her, neither with a smile nor frown. That was the thing about Sam. When he didn't want to show any emotion, he was good at it.

"I was just telling Corrie and Jenny I need about two minutes with you. Can we talk in your office?"

"Is Mrs. Norris here yet?" Sam asked Jenny.

"No, not yet," she said.

He motioned Alicia down the hall to his office. When they went inside his office and closed the door, Corrie's stomach did a nosedive.

Jenny muttered, "I wish she'd leave him alone."

"Maybe he doesn't *want* to be left alone," Corrie murmured. Maybe underneath it all he really did love Alicia and with a bit of persuading from her, they'd be back together. What did that say about Sam? That he was willing to forgive? Or that he was willing to compromise his values to be with a woman like Alicia.

Corrie might have stayed spruced up since her makeover, but she could never compete with a woman like that, whether Sam liked her freckles or not.

She wouldn't stand around waiting to see what happened.

Seeing Eric's next patient coming through the door, she motioned to the man with his dalmatian and took him to an empty exam room.

After Corrie jotted down pre-exam notes on the chart and Eric took over, she went to the kennel. She needed a few minutes just to pull herself together. After she petted a few of the animals and talked to them, she washed up and went back to the reception area.

Sam was escorting Mrs. Wellington and her Persian into an exam room. He glanced at Corrie impatiently. "You have to tell me if you need a break. We're backed up in the reception area. A poodle and Mrs. Wellington's cat almost had a duel."

Sudden tears came to Corrie's eyes and there were many things she could say, like, *I'm not the one who had a conference with my ex-fiancée*. But Sam was her boss. And their schedule was tight because of taking an emergency patient earlier. Instead of saying something she shouldn't, instead of making the situation worse, instead of letting Sam see her upset, she turned her back on him and went to the unisex bathroom down the hall and locked the door. She had to pull herself together whether they were behind schedule or not.

She'd no sooner braced her hands on either side of the sink when a loud knock punctuated her already scrambled thoughts.

"Corrie, it's Sam. Open up."

"I'm in the bathroom, Sam. That's a private place."

There was silence for a few moments until he asked, "Are you all right?"

No, she wasn't, but she wasn't going to tell him that. "I'm fine. Just give me a minute and you won't get any farther behind."

He rattled the knob. "Let me in, Corrie. You're hiding in there."

Hiding? He thought she was hiding? She unlocked the door and opened it. "I am *not* hiding. I'm just trying to pull myself together so I don't make a fool of myself. But you're doing a good job of making a fool of both of us."

Eric was standing at the end of the hall and so was Jenny. She could hear a dog barking in the reception area and maybe someone else was listening, too.

After Sam glanced over his shoulder, he nudged her inside and shut the door. The bathroom had been equipped for efficiency, not luxury.

Sam was almost nose to nose with her and she felt claustrophobic. "What are you doing? There are patients out there to see," she said.

"I'm sorry I snapped at you."

To her dismay, she felt close to tears again. She took a deep breath.

As if Sam sensed only complete disclosure would lessen the tension between them, he admitted, "Alicia wanted to go to lunch."

"This isn't any of my business, Sam." Her voice was shaky and she hated that he could see how upset she was.

"The hell it isn't. If you think I made love with you when I still had feelings for Alicia Walker, you're *wrong*. There's nothing left and that's what I told her. We aren't going to have any lunches or dinners, or even friendly chats. What she did was just too enormous for me even to see around. Alicia is out of my life."

"But do you really want her out of your life, Sam? If you do, then why were you short with me?"

Reaching toward her, he fingered a few of her curls and then shook his head. "You're not who I thought you were, Corrie. You're this complicated woman who surrounds herself with a thick, high wall, independence painted all over it. I'm worried about how that will affect my relationship with my son or daughter."

She could see he was being sincere. He usually was and that was one of the things she loved about him. "I won't keep you from your child, but I don't want to feel as if you're running my life."

"Is it running your life to tell you what I think is best?"

"No, but it *is* running my life if you always expect me to *do* what you think is best."

His lips suddenly turned up at the corners. They were such sexy, masculine lips. She wanted them on hers again. She wanted to be in his arms again. She wanted him to make love to her again, yet she couldn't let that happen.

In spite of what he said, he had wounds from Alicia and Corrie didn't think they were healed. She had her own wounds. The scars just meant she'd put everything behind her, but she'd never stop being affected by them, just as Sam wouldn't.

"We're two stubborn, self-determined people. Why didn't I notice this in the past three years you were working for me?" Sam asked.

"Because then I wasn't carrying your baby. Now I am."

His smile slipped away. "We'll figure this out, Corrie. We have to for the baby's sake."

Yes, they did. For the baby's sake.

On Saturday afternoon as Sam drove down the lane to the Klinedinst farm, he remembered Corrie's excitement when he'd phoned her, asking her to join him for dinner at Nathan and Sara's.

She'd explained she was at the farm, looking over the property. It had so many possibilities.

Sam felt as if he had a lead ball in his stomach and he didn't know why. Maybe he didn't want to envision Corrie's life at the farm if the homeless shelter was established. Maybe he was jealous of Nathan and the fact that he was a dad in every sense of the word.

Exactly what was Sam going to be? A role model that his son thought of as more of a benevolent friend than a father? A visitor who lived on the fringes of his child's life?

Wasn't that what he'd intended all along? No relationship complications with a woman. No chains that bind. No vows that could be broken.

It had sounded good in theory.

Colin Bancroft's BMW was parked in front of the

detached garage. Sam pulled up beside it, noticing the tall firs to the left of the house, the snow-covered fields stretching as far as his eye could see. Outbuildings had been torn down long ago. It had been many years since this was actually a working farm. But Corrie would have enough property that she could build barns and rescue horses, too, if she wanted to. And she would want to.

Sam climbed out of his van. His boots crunched on the mixture of snow and gravel as he made his way to the two-story farmhouse with a side porch, a bay window and a second-story gable. The clapboard house needed to be modernized with siding, maybe even new windows. But that would be Corrie's concern, not his. *If* she decided to take the position.

The doorbell didn't work. When he knocked, he got no answer. Trying the knob, he pushed open the door.

The house was empty. Stepping over the threshold, he saw that the living room had dull wood floors and flowered wallpaper that had yellowed with the years. Both hinted at the house's age. He could hear voices coming from beyond French doors. He went that way and heard Corrie saying to Bancroft, "This window area would be a perfect place for floor-to-ceiling cat condos. They'd love the sunlight."

Bancroft was peering out the bay window. "Would you fence in the yard area? Or would you build dog runs?"

"I have a lot of research to finish before I even contemplate doing this."

Bancroft gave a dry chuckle. "I have a feeling you've already contemplated doing this."

Sam did, too, noticing Corrie's color was high and her eyes were bright with enthusiasm.

"Making plans?" he asked as nonchalantly as he could manage as he walked closer to them.

Corrie spun around. "Hi, Sam. I didn't hear you come in."

"These old houses with their plastered walls and wide windowsills don't let sound carry like new houses do."

"What do you think of the house?" Corrie asked him.

He really had to be careful how he answered her. He had the feeling she didn't want anyone squashing the ideas running through her mind. "You need to have some work done before you turn this into a shelter."

"What kind of work?"

"The practical kind. You need to make the building low-maintenance. You also need to ask a few questions, like how old is the furnace? Will you soon need a new roof? Is the plumbing adequate? If you're going to live here, you might have to turn the upstairs into an apartment."

"I'm going to wander outside a bit," Bancroft murmured, perceptively sensing a discussion brewing.

"We'll be out in a couple of minutes," Corrie assured him.

After Bancroft crossed to the front door, Sam asked Corrie, "Have you thought about having a crying baby upstairs and barking dogs and meowing cats downstairs?"

Corrie moved away from the windows and closer to him. He caught the scent of her perfume, the one she wore when she wasn't working. She was dressed for winter today in a navy and light-blue turtleneck, pale-blue corduroy slacks. The house was barely heated, only enough so the pipes wouldn't freeze. Corrie's yellow parka was unzipped. It was as bright as the sunshine outside. She always seemed to bring the sun into a room with her along with the warmth that came from caring about whatever she did. But now that warmth was replaced with determination. When he thought how close they'd been that Sunday when they'd made love and how far apart they seemed to be right now, his chest tightened.

"I know how you feel about the project and me being involved in it," she said with resignation.

"I have nothing against a shelter for animals," he protested. "I have nothing against you being part of it. But you being pregnant and being part of it, and you being a new mom and being part of it have me worried."

After she studied him, she asked, "Have you ever known me to be impulsive and unrealistic?"

"You're usually a planner," he admitted.

"Exactly. And I'm practical, too. That's why I'm thinking about taking the job as director rather than being a live-in doggie and kitty housemother. I believe I could do a good job, but I want to make sure of that before I give Mr. Bancroft a definite yes."

Sam felt as if Corrie were slipping away from him and that was ridiculous. "You'll definitely have a busy life, busier than it is now."

"I'll have a full life, Sam, and a vocation rather than just a job. I've always wanted to take in animals and protect them. Now I have my chance." She gave him a smile. "If I do this, I'll need a vet on-call. Do you want to apply for the position?"

Instead of becoming defensive, she was trying to convince him cooperation was better than confrontation. Reason told him that was true. "I'll consider it. But I have to ask you something, Corrie. You want me to be this child's role model. What if I want to be more than that?"

He expected Corrie to flare up, but she didn't. Rather she asked, "What kind of father do you *want* to be?"

Suddenly he knew without a doubt. "I want joint custody."

Corrie's eyes grew wide. Then her shoulders squared and her chin lifted.

Sam knew he was going to have a fight on his hands.

However, instead of arguing with him, Corrie zipped up her parka. "We'd better go."

"What about joint custody?"

"Can we just table it for now?"

"Table it?"

"Yes. This isn't something we can settle with one discussion. And the truth is, I need to think about it before I can talk to you about it. I have a lot to mull over right now. My dad's coming to visit tomorrow for a week. I'm going to have to deal with him. Because we have some time, I'd like to just set this discussion aside for now."

Sam knew he only had an inkling of what was going on inside Corrie. She wanted full custody and he'd probably thrown her for a loop. He also knew she didn't want to deal with her dad, and if he was going to be in close proximity for a week, she was probably worried about handling the situation. Shirley's legacy was also a weight on her shoulders. He could almost feel the invisible walls Corrie was surrounding herself with so that she could deal with all of it.

He wanted to reach through those walls and give her a helping hand if she'd take it. He didn't want her to see him as the enemy.

Draping his arm around her shoulders, he wanted to pull her into his arms. He longed to kiss her until she came around to his way of thinking. He understood that right now, however, that would not be the best thing to do.

At first she tensed. But then as he gave her a squeeze, she turned to him with a grateful smile. With his face so close to hers he could see every one of her freckles, and he remembered freckles in many more intimate places.

Blanking out those pictures, he assured her, "We'll table a joint-custody discussion until your dad goes back to Minneapolis. But then we're going to figure this out."

Chapter Eleven

"Are you going to stay in the same room with me for more than two minutes?" George Edwards asked his daughter as she returned to her town house after a walk with Jasper.

Her father had been here for about four hours and already Corrie felt guilty. She wasn't the one who had anything to feel guilty about. Granted, being with him was uncomfortable and she wanted to escape that, but she thought she'd been doing a good job of smiling and chatting, even though she'd fluttered from one thing to the next since he'd arrived.

Unzipping her parka, she hung it in the living-room closet. She could feel his gaze on her and considered how he'd changed in the past few years. There were more lines on his face than there used to be. At almost sixty, his brown hair had thinned and now rimmed his balding head. Lean most of his life, he'd gained a few pounds, but the weight gain just made him look more substantial.

As an answer to his question, she replied, "I'm going to cook dinner…a stir-fry. Do you like stir-fry?"

"Sure, as long as we can sit down and have a conversation over dinner."

Instead of running off to the kitchen to start supper, she sank onto the arm of the chair. "What do you want to have a conversation about?"

"Why I'm here."

Rehashing the old baggage made her defensive. "I thought you came for a visit."

"I did, but something pushed me into it." Her father motioned for her to sit in the chair instead of on its arm. "Settle in for a couple of minutes, will you, Corrie? You look like you're going to fly away."

Doing as her dad asked, she sat on the chair but didn't relax into it. She waited.

"I had a scare recently. I thought I was having a heart attack."

With the tightening in her throat, a little voice whispered, *He's the only family you have left.*

"I got into an argument with one of my customers over a bill. I had chest pains, at least that's what I thought they were. I can't tell you how scared I was when I thought I was having a heart attack. That whole life-flashing-in-front-of-your eyes business? It's true. I was lying there in the E.R. having blood work done, getting an EKG, and I looked at the scope of my life. I wasn't pleased with a lot of it, starting with what happened with your mother. I never should have left her."

"That was your choice." Corrie tried to keep her voice

from being cold, but she'd always detached herself from these emotions. She knew how her mother had suffered, how she'd cried, how she'd hurt. She'd loved her husband. Not only had he stopped loving her, but he hadn't told her he'd stopped loving her. Instead he went out and found someone else. Then he'd left and divorced her, pushed her aside as if she hadn't mattered at all. Corrie had been there for every minute of that and had experienced it with her mom. Erasing the memories wasn't a possibility.

"You told Mom you didn't love her anymore." One day when Corrie had found her mother crying, that's what she'd confided to her daughter.

George wove his hands together and dropped them between his knees. "I told her that, but it wasn't true. I just thought I loved Elaine more. I thought she was the one who could make me happy."

"No one can *make* you happy, Dad. You have to make yourself happy."

Looking sad and regretful, he nodded. "I found that out. Elaine didn't need me like your mother did. If two people don't need each other, what point is there in being together?"

Although Corrie wanted to refute that conclusion, she thought about it first. There was an element of truth to it—whether the bonds were friendship or love. She didn't want to need anyone so she was alone most of the time. She hadn't had a real woman friend since she'd moved to Rapid Creek. Sara was quickly becoming that friend because they had a lot in common. Maybe not on the surface, but inside. Sara had support from her husband—he loved her deeply, that was obvious—but she needed Corrie, too, for that bonding only women can give each other. And Corrie felt the same need.

Then there was Sam. She didn't want to need him. But the problem was, even though she felt she was self-sufficient, she did.

"Mom *learned* not to need you. She learned how to make herself happy." But deep down, Corrie knew her mother hadn't been happy. After her divorce, she'd longed for the relationship with her husband she'd once had.

"Elaine and your mom weren't at all alike. I thought she was what I was looking for. But I was stupid and just fell into the adventure of new love."

Except for a few confidences in her most vulnerable moments, her mother hadn't discussed her divorce. "Did you ever tell Mom you were wrong?"

"No, I didn't, because I knew she'd never forgive me. I knew once I'd broken her trust, she'd never trust me again."

That was true enough. Her mother had once warned her that if a man was unfaithful once, he'd be unfaithful again. Was that really true?

"Will you be honest with me about something?" she asked.

"I'll try."

"If you and Mom had gotten back together, would you have stayed faithful for the rest of your life?"

"I don't know. That's as honest as I can be."

That wasn't good enough for Corrie. If she made a promise, she intended to keep it, no matter what. Why couldn't men be the same? Why couldn't her dad be sure he'd never stray again.

"Honey, you've always wanted me to be perfect. Few parents can live up to that. I can't pretend I'm not who I am. I could just tell you what you want to hear, but you asked for honesty. When I look back over my life, I regret so many things. But what I regret most is the distance between *us*."

That took Corrie by surprise.

His gaze never wavered from hers. "I know you felt if you had a relationship with me, you'd be betraying your mother. But isn't it time we get beyond all that? Isn't it time we really become father and daughter again?"

She couldn't give him an answer to that, so instead she went another route. "You said you thought you were having a heart attack. What was wrong?"

"I have an ulcer and acid reflux. The condition can mimic a heart attack. I've had all the tests, seen too many doctors. I have to watch my diet and take medication."

"If you need special food while you're here, just let me know—"

He interrupted, "Corrie, I'm not worried about what I'm going to eat while I'm here. I'm worried about you being uncomfortable with me, afraid to talk to me. How can I get through that resentment you've always used as a barrier between us?"

"I can't just pretend you didn't leave! I can't just pretend that didn't hurt."

"I know that. But can we can put it aside? Maybe if we can have a real conversation, it won't seem so important any more."

"What do you want to have a real conversation about?" she asked warily.

He leaned against the sofa cushions and stretched his arm along the back. "Tell me about work. When I ask you about it on the phone, you tell me it's fine. I don't even know exactly what you do."

"As a veterinary assistant, I see the animals first, take

down any necessary information, weigh them and help the vets in any way I can. I enjoy it, but I guess I've always wanted to be more and finish my degree."

"You still can. If you need money—"

Her pride had always been more important than taking any help from her father. Or maybe her mother's pride had been more important. Corrie wasn't sure. "I could, but something else has come up."

"Here in Rapid Creek?"

"Yes." She told him about Shirley Klinedinst and Colin Bancroft coming to her with the offer. She ended up with, "I went to Shirley's house yesterday and ideas are just floating in left and right. I think I'd do a good job as the director."

"So what's keeping you from taking it?"

She hadn't intended to tell him yet. In fact, she hadn't been sure she'd tell him at all. At least not on this visit. But this conversation had just led into her news.

"I'm pregnant."

Her father went altogether still and she could tell he was trying hard not to react.

"I'm not sure what to say. I don't want to say the wrong thing. Are you dating someone seriously?"

"It's not like that, Dad. I decided I wanted to have a baby without being married. I want a child and I want to be a mom. So I used a sperm donor. I did it through artificial insemination."

"Did you go to a clinic? You chose someone out of a catalog?" He looked stricken by the thought.

"No. Someone at work. He's a friend. He donated his sperm." She felt a bit embarrassed talking about this with her dad, but she shouldn't be. They were facts…only facts.

"And you're worried the job will be too much with a baby?"

"I don't know. I'd like to think I can handle both."

"If anyone can handle both, Corrie Edwards, you can. You're the most independent woman I've ever seen, and the most competent."

"How do you know? I mean, it's not like we're around each other very much."

"I know. But I was at your graduation even though you didn't know it. I knew you graduated with honors not only from high school but from college. Afterward, you could have stayed at veterinary school and finished your training, but instead, you nursed your mother. A weak woman doesn't do that."

After the silence between them started to become uncomfortable, he suggested, "If you really intend to finish your degree, maybe you should relocate to Minneapolis. Live with me after your baby's born and go back to school."

"You wouldn't get any sleep," she joked, surprised and touched by the invitation.

"I'm slowing down. My hours are more my own. I really could help with your baby. I remember taking care of *you*."

Corrie and her dad had been close once. She remembered him carrying her to bed, roller-skating with her, reading her stories. So many emotions ran together she didn't know what to do with them all. Could she become friends with her father after all the troubled water that had flowed between them?

She rose to her feet. "I'm going to start supper."

"Corrie?"

She stopped in the doorway to the kitchen.

"We have a week to get to know each other again. I'm

sorry if I tried to do it all in one day. Over supper we can stick to the weather if that's what you want to talk about."

The weather would give them a nice break. But the weather wouldn't catch them up on each other's lives. Maybe they could find neutral territory in between.

On Tuesday morning, Sam was working with Corrie less than five minutes when he realized something was on her mind. She helped him prep animals for surgery and assisted him expertly as always. But he was so attuned to her now, so aware of the way she avoided or met his eyes that he was sure she was mulling over something. Her dad's visit? Her job at the clinic? Having the baby? Working with him?

It was almost one o'clock before he finished with surgery. He knew Corrie would be watching their post-surgery patients closely while he called their owners to let them know their animals were doing fine.

"Did you eat lunch?" Sam asked her as she came into the lounge.

"I wasn't hungry. I made a big breakfast for Dad."

"Did you eat it, too?"

"Actually, I did. I'm ravenous in the mornings when I get up. No signs of morning sickness yet. It's this time of day that I—" She shrugged. "Lose my energy and feel a little queasy."

"Then take a few minutes. We're caught up for the moment."

"I have to make the midafternoon notations on charts."

"Corrie, it can wait." After his gaze locked to hers, she was the first to look away.

"I take it your dad arrived okay? How's it going?"

She paced over to the window, peered out, and answered his question. "He wants to bridge the distance between us."

"He said that?"

"Yeah. He plunged right in on the day he arrived. But I'm not sure how to react. I'm not sure how I feel. Have you forgiven *your* mother for leaving?"

"You start out with the hard ones," he teased gently, then went to her because this discussion wasn't one to have with a room between them.

"You don't have to answer that," she murmured.

He had the feeling Corrie might bolt on him, and he didn't want her going anywhere. Standing by her shoulder, noticing the sun catch the redder strands in her hair, he responded, "I don't know if I made a conscious decision to forgive her. I was the youngest, so my memories were the vaguest. One day she was there and the next she wasn't. My dad was angry and bitter. Ben, Nathan and I felt bad. We banded together to try to do anything we could to make life easier for him. From what I remember about our mother, she wasn't particularly happy. She talked a lot about life in London and going to school there. We all know she didn't particularly enjoy being a homemaker and chores like the laundry and cooking were duties she felt she had to perform. I was in high school when our dad told us that she'd died a few years before in a skiing accident. When I found that out, I think I just shut out the fact we'd ever had a mother. Forgiveness never entered into it."

Corrie switched her attention from the scenery outside to him. "My dad said he was sorry he left my mother."

"I think some people always want what they can't

have, or they think they know what they want and they really don't. Or else they don't have the courage to fix what they mess up."

"I just wish…" Corrie began.

"What do you wish?" he asked when she stopped.

"I wish I knew what my mother would want me to do now."

"I think you know what that is."

In all the time he'd known Corrie, he'd never seen her this vulnerable. But her eyes became shiny when she said, "I guess I wish Dad had fought harder after he and Mom separated to keep in contact with me. I didn't want anything to do with him and he just accepted that. He accepted it for years, and during that time my resentment grew. But now, maybe it *is* time to let it all go." She gave him a small smile. "I think he's excited about the idea of being a granddad."

"You told him about the artificial insemination?"

"Yes, and that you were the donor."

"Am I going to get to meet your dad?" He asked the question lightly, but it was suddenly important that he did.

"If you'd like to. We're going to the play at the Little Theater tomorrow night. I think there are still tickets available if you'd want to go."

"I'll see if I can get a seat. What's your father doing while you're at work?"

"Actually he drove to Grand Rapids today and won't be back until late tonight. He has a friend who lives there and he hasn't seen him in a long time."

Sam had been restraining himself from touching Corrie but now that restraint broke and he reached out and stroked her cheek. "How would you like to come to my place tonight? I'll cook you dinner."

"You don't have to do that."

"I want to. We can just kick back, relax, watch a video. Nothing heavy."

"Do you mean that?"

"I do. It will be just you, me, Patches and Jasper hanging out." His hand settled on her shoulder. When his thumb found a freckle on her neck and circled it, he felt her tremble.

"That sounds wonderful," she said a bit shakily. "What can I bring?"

"Just you." He might have kissed her then, he might have taken her into his arms, and they might have made love again on the couch, but he'd never know because the bell in the reception area rang, and he guessed Mr. Thompson had come to pick up Rochester, a boxer who had had minor surgery today.

As Corrie moved away from him, gave him a smile and left the lounge, Sam knew no other vet assistant could replace her.

No other woman could replace her? Because she was carrying his child?

Absolutely.

Tonight he hoped she could relax around him. Tonight, he hoped she'd let her walls down and invite him in.

"Can I help?" Corrie had entered Sam's apartment a few moments before. While she shed her jacket, Jasper was already tugging on a chew toy with Patches in the living room.

"Everything's almost ready." Sam added a pat of butter to the vegetables then looked over at her. When their eyes met, her heart beat so fast she could hardly get her breath.

There was something in his expression that made her feel warm and tingly, and very glad she was here.

"You can grab the salad from the refrigerator. Once I take out the meat loaf, we'll be all set."

Telling herself this was Sam, she was here to relax and just have a fun time, she crossed to the refrigerator. "Where did you learn to cook meat loaf?"

"It's my dad's recipe. He made it every Thursday night and we always looked forward to it."

After she set the salad on the table, Sam brought the main course to the table and motioned for her to sit. "Having dinner together was something Dad insisted we should do as often as we could. It was hard sometimes, particularly when we were playing sports, but Sunday dinner especially was sacred and nothing interfered."

"That's nice," Corrie murmured, thinking of her and her mom, the long silences after her dad left, the companionship as they'd gotten used to living without him.

"I should cook more," she admitted. "I eat too much Chinese takeout. But that will stop once I have a baby. I want to make my own baby food."

"You're going to be a natural mother."

"As natural as I can be."

"Does that mean labor and delivery, too?"

"Sure does. I might even look into having a midwife."

"You're not serious."

"Yes, I am." She knew exactly why he was frowning. "It's safe, Sam, really."

"I'd have to be convinced of that."

She reached across the table and touched his hand. "I've done a lot of research on the Internet and I plan to speak to someone in town. I'll give you the number if you'd like."

"We can always go together."

She pulled her hand back. "Yes, I guess we could." But did she want to? Did she want Sam to be involved in *everything?*

Over dinner, Sam took the conversation in a different direction. He told her stories about him and his brothers when they were kids and he elicited information from her about her life in Minneapolis. They were sitting around the corner from each other and every once in a while their knees brushed. Sam didn't move his leg away and she tried to steady her pulse. He looked so sexy tonight in jeans and a chambray shirt, the sleeves rolled up. His sneakers had seen a lot of walks with Patches and she loved his unpretentiousness. She loved him.

But that confused her and upset her. Sometimes she found it downright impossible to believe she was going to have his baby. Maybe that was because of the way they'd done it. If they made love again...

She wasn't seriously considering it, was she?

"What just crossed your mind?" he asked her.

Embarrassed, she looked down at her plate. "Nothing."

He tipped her chin up with his thumb. "You're a terrible liar. Whatever it was, it added some extra sparkle to your eyes."

When she still didn't say anything, he let her off the hook. "Dessert now or later?"

"Later."

They were clearing the table together when it happened. Sam was so close Corrie couldn't think straight. He was wearing aftershave tonight. Every time she inhaled it, she noticed his strong jaw, the line of his lips, and her insides felt like mush. She reached for a napkin at the same time he did. He was slow to pull away. They bumped into each other at the sink. He laughed and she did, too. But the laughter faded away into unbearable awareness.

When she returned to the table, he watched her and she felt as if he were seeing her naked again. She imagined *him* naked and her face felt hot. He picked up the silverware and she reached for the glasses. She dropped one and water spilled, soaking the tablecloth and dripping onto the chair.

She backed away and murmured, "I'm so sorry."

Sam didn't seem to care about the spilled water. He was there in front of her, holding her shoulders, kissing her. All of their pent-up desire caught fire.

His lips were hot, his tongue possessive and his hands? She wanted to feel them everywhere. When her fingers fumbled with his shirt buttons, he helped her. As his hands tunneled under her sweater and lifted it over her head, she unfastened her bra. She had worn a pale-blue lacy one tonight that matched her bikini panties. She hadn't consciously dressed for Sam, had she? She hadn't known this was going to happen.

They were so eager for each other that they didn't move into the living-room area or the bedroom. Once Sam removed his boots, jeans and briefs, he swung a chair around, sat on it and watched her finish removing her clothes. When he opened his arms to her, she straddled him and sank down onto his lap. Where they'd bantered and talked before, there were no words now, only hunger and the all-consuming need to feel Sam inside of her. He nibbled at her collarbone then took her breast in his hand and brought his lips to it. The sensations that tugged at her womb were erotic and exciting as she cried out and then moved restlessly on his lap seeking fulfillment.

He read the signal and understood it. Holding her hips, he entered her. The sheer completion Corrie felt shook her. The words *I love you* almost slipped from her lips, but he was kissing her, holding her tightly and moving inside her. She rocked back and forth on him. She was lost in Sam's touch and taste, the feel of him hot, hard and swollen where she needed him most. The tantalizing sensations increased like a storm building in ferocity till the lightning and thunder finally released a torrent of rain. Her orgasm poured over her and she held on to Sam. When his final release hit, he broke their kiss, held her tightly, and shuddered against her. They breathed in unison as they let their world right itself again.

Then, as Corrie opened her eyes and looked into Sam's, she didn't know if her world would ever be right. She longed to believe that he wanted her and desired her and saw her as a woman he could find happiness with. Yet, as her breathing became normal, as her body cooled down and she shivered, even though she was still joined to Sam, doubts gnawed at her.

Sam had told Alicia they didn't have a future, but was he truly over her? Or was he looking for someone merely to distract him from having his dreams dashed? Was he having sex with her because she was convenient? Worse yet, did he have an ulterior motive? He'd told her he wanted joint custody. Did he see this as a means to get it?

"What?" he asked, strain in his voice.

She slid off of him, grabbed for a towel, muttered, "I'll be right back," and went straight to the bathroom. It was only when she'd gotten there that she realized she'd forgotten her clothes. Sam Barclay scrambled her brains, kept her off balance, made her unsure. She turned on the water and leaned on the sink.

There was a loud knock on the door. "Corrie, I have your clothes."

She couldn't tell him to go away when she was in his bathroom, in his apartment, had just made love with him again. She took a deep breath and then opened the door.

He was holding her sweater and pants, and the blue lacy underwear was on top. "I thought you might need these."

When she took them from him, her hands brushed his arm and the electricity that had brought them together sparked again.

"I didn't ask you here tonight for that," Sam admitted gruffly. "I really did just want to hang out with you."

"Everything between us is all mixed up. I don't know what your motives are, or what I want or even if we should be getting involved."

"What my motives are?"

"You told me you want joint custody. What better way to get it than what just happened?"

She'd rarely seen Sam angry, but he looked angry now. "I would never use sex to persuade you to think my way."

"Even if it's not intentional—"

"I'm serious, Corrie. Unintentionally, intentionally, not ever. I don't know where the chemistry between us came from, but wherever it did, it's potent. It seems to have a mind of its own. Maybe it will go away as quickly as it erupted. I don't know. It sure doesn't feel like that right now."

He'd pulled on his jeans, zipped the fly but hadn't buttoned them. She could tell he had an erection again and she didn't know what to say. She still wanted him, too.

Swearing, he stepped out of the bathroom and shut the door.

Corrie sat on the closed commode, her clothes in hand, not knowing what to do next.

Chapter Twelve

Sam hadn't *planned* to have sex with Corrie again.

As he sat in the theater, craning his neck every few minutes to spot Corrie and her dad, he was beginning to believe his subconscious ran his life!

His need for Corrie had been so hungry and hot, so fast and furious, that he'd lost control of it.

The lights blinked, signaling the play would soon begin. Maybe Corrie had convinced her dad meeting Sam *wasn't* a good idea.

He spotted movement in the aisle on the other side of the theater—Corrie and her dad hurrying to their seats. The theater went dark and Sam counted the minutes until intermission.

Why was meeting Corrie's dad such a big deal?

As soon as the lights in the theater blinked back on at intermission, Sam lost no time making his way to the

row where Corrie and her father sat. He wasn't sure
what he saw in Corrie's eyes as her dad stood and shook
his hand. She seemed uncertain these days and that
wasn't at all like Corrie.

George Edwards looked Sam up and down. No one
wore suits in Rapid Creek unless they were attending a
funeral, a wedding…or a Valentine's Day dance. George
was wearing a suit. The way the man was appraising
Sam's sweater and jeans made Sam feel like a teenager
taking a girl on a date for the first time.

"I hope you're enjoying the play, Mr. Edwards." Sam
thought he'd start out with something easy.

"I am. It's amazing what your local talent can do."

Sam wasn't sure where to go from there. Corrie was
still silent and he guessed she was going to make him sink
or swim on his own. How did you get into a subject like
a baby in a place like this?

"I'd be glad to take you both for coffee and dessert
when the production's over," Sam said. The conversation
could be more casual.

George patted his belly. "Oh, I can't eat dessert this
time of night. I've become very health conscious, even
joined the gym."

Sam felt as if he was stuck in the middle of nowhere
and Corrie wasn't throwing him a lifeline. He tried again.
"Maybe you'd like to visit the clinic tomorrow. Corrie
could show you around."

"I'll be going ice-fishing tomorrow. And I think my
daughter will be glad to get me out of her hair."

At this Corrie shook her head. "You haven't been any
trouble, Dad, and I know it's been boring for you while

I've been at work all day." She said to Sam, "He brought all his gear along. Tell him about your family's cabin."

George patted his daughter on the shoulder. "You said you were thirsty. Why don't you get something to drink while Sam and I talk."

Corrie gave Sam an Is-that-okay? look. He nodded. If he had to get to know Corrie's dad this way, that's what he'd do. Ice-fishing was safe enough.

But ice-fishing wasn't the topic her father pursued.

"What made you decide to be a sperm donor for my daughter? Did you get paid for it?"

To Sam's relief, no other playgoers were within earshot. Sam's shoulders squared, his spine straightened and he decided he wasn't going to be defensive with this man, he was just going to tell it like it was. "No fee was involved. This had nothing to do with money."

George shook his head. "What was in it for *you?*"

He wasn't giving Corrie's dad his life history when he felt as if he was walking up a steep road with no chance of a meeting of minds at the end of it. "I've always wanted to be a dad. I admire my own father. And I've watched my brother with his son."

"But you won't really *be* a dad, will you? Corrie told me the two of you are friends and you're her boss. That doesn't go very far when decisions about the future have to be made. You have no personal investment here. It's not as if you and my daughter are involved."

He and Corrie were involved all right. A lot more than this man knew. And Sam was feeling more and more involved every day. Because of the baby? He wasn't even sure about that.

Corrie's father went on, "She told me about the job offer from that lawyer."

"I think she wants to take it."

"Yes, I think she does, too. But that would be accepting a great responsibility at an important time of her life. I made another suggestion."

Sam's instincts told him he wasn't going to like this suggestion at all.

"Corrie and I are settling some matters on this trip. And the truth of it is, I want to be a father to her in a way I was never able to be. I'd like to be a good granddad to this baby. She and I are mending fences and I don't want that to stop when I leave. She doesn't really have a lot of ties here, the way I see it, so I suggested she move back to Minneapolis."

Back to Minneapolis? Sam's heart almost stopped.

"She shouldn't be revving up her life right now, but winding it down a little. As her pregnancy progresses, she'll need some time off, not new projects. If she returns to Minneapolis with me, she can finish up her degree. After the baby's born, I can help her. When she's ready, she can work for a veterinary practice there or start up her own. I could subsidize her. She wouldn't take any money from me for college, but now I think she'll see it all differently."

Independent Corrie depending on her father? Could her mind-set really have changed this much in a week?

Sam had to find out if she was seriously thinking about leaving Rapid Creek.

Corrie's dad dismissed further conversation with Sam when he said, "I'm going to find the men's room before I have to sit through the second half."

While George headed in one direction, Sam veered

toward the lobby. Corrie was examining the performance schedule for the upcoming season.

He tapped her shoulder and when she turned toward him he asked, "Are you seriously thinking about living in Minneapolis?"

Usually Corrie showed her emotions. Even though she was sometimes guarded, he could tell what she was thinking. But right now he couldn't.

"My dad has suggested it," she replied cautiously.

"You'd live with him and go to school until the baby's born?"

She shrugged, but her gaze stayed on his face. "That's one option."

"What about the shelter?"

"I'm still considering that, too. I got the feeling you thought that was something I shouldn't undertake."

"You have to make your own decisions about your life, Corrie. But if you move back to Minneapolis, how much am I going to see my son or daughter?"

He thought he saw disappointment in her eyes and he didn't know why. He was ready to take over his responsibilities for being a dad and she wanted to steal those away from him.

"This isn't settled yet, Sam. I'm thinking about what's practical and what's not." Again she searched his face as if she were looking for something important.

The lights in the theater dimmed, announcing that intermission was over. "I have to get back to my seat. We can talk about this later."

"When, later? After you make up your mind?"

"No. After my dad goes back to Minneapolis. That's what we agreed, wasn't it?"

Sam knew that's what he'd told her they'd do. But now the discussion seemed more urgent.

With a last look at him, Corrie left the lobby to join her dad.

As the playgoers milled around him, Sam watched Corrie's back, watched the curls bobbing on her shoulders, remembered the sex they'd had and the way he'd felt afterward.

He turned toward the theater doors and pushed one open. He couldn't sit through the end of the play, knowing that if Corrie moved to Minneapolis, she'd have sole custody.

He had to do something about that.

"Corrie's thinking about moving to Minneapolis to be near her dad." Sam ended his explanation to his brother Ben, still not believing Corrie would consider leaving Rapid Creek. Hadn't they established an understanding? Hadn't they developed a bond of friendship? When they'd had sex, he'd felt as if he'd been on top of the world…invincible. And he'd known he could be the best dad and Corrie the best mom that the world had ever seen.

Sam didn't quite catch the words that Ben uttered, but he could imagine what they were.

"Do you have anything in writing?" his brother asked curtly.

"No."

"Did you consult a lawyer there?"

"No."

"How likely is it that she *is* going to move?"

"I really don't know. I brought up the idea of joint custody last weekend and she seemed upset by it."

"I guess so, if she thought she was going to have sole custody. Sam, you've gone about this all wrong."

Ben's "I told you so" didn't help, even if he hadn't said it in so many words. "If I see a lawyer now, do you think it will help?"

"Only if you can get decent terms in writing that she'll sign. What are the chances of that?"

"Corrie's not a vindictive woman, or even a selfish one."

"Isn't it selfish for her to move to Minneapolis?"

"Not if she wants to be near her dad." Sam knew exactly what Ben was thinking, because he'd thought about it, too. "This isn't like our mother leaving without a thought for any of us."

"Corrie's not thinking about *you*."

"She's thinking about the baby. She's thinking about what she needs to do to raise the child the best way she can."

"Dammit, Sam, selfish is selfish. She's going to do what's right for her, even if that means leaving you out in the cold. You have to protect yourself. Make an appointment with a lawyer as soon as you can and get papers drawn up with liberal visitation rights no matter how far away she is or you are."

"Do you think I should consult with a lawyer who specializes in custody issues? I could ask Sara, but that's not her area, and I don't particularly want to draw her into the middle of this. She and Corrie have become friends."

"It's a good thing I'm still at the office," Ben said. "Hold on a minute. I'm going to make a call to a family law attorney I know. He works with lawyers from all areas of the country. Do you want me to call you back or do you want to hold?"

"I'll hold." Sam glanced at the clock above the sink.

Midnight here—eleven in Albuquerque. All of Ben's friends must work late.

Sam paced until Patches, finally disturbed from his bed by his master's unusual behavior, shook himself awake and trotted over to Sam, pacing the apartment with him.

The thought of Corrie leaving bounced around inside Sam's head until he couldn't think of anything else. He'd thought she'd wanted the job at the animal shelter. Sure, there could be problems with that. But they could solve the problems. If she was in Minneapolis, he couldn't just drop in on her. They wouldn't see each other in the grocery store. They couldn't walk their dogs together.

"Sam?"

Ben was finally back on the line. "Do you have a pen?"

Snatching a pen from the counter and his grocery list tablet from the refrigerator, he said, "Ready. Go ahead."

Ben rattled off a name and phone number and then the name of the attorney who had given him the information. "Jonas is going to call and leave a message for Sean Curtis so he'll know who you are when you call. Phone him tomorrow morning."

"I'll drive to Minneapolis if I have to."

"You might be able to handle all of it over the phone. Curtis can fax you the papers when they're finished. If I were you, I'd pay him extra to get them done quickly. Don't let this ride, Sam. You've got to stay on top of it."

Sam suddenly realized there were two reasons to do as Ben suggested. One, yes, he did want to be able to see his son or daughter as often as he could. But two? Maybe if he showed Corrie he was serious about joint custody she'd reconsider moving to Minneapolis. After all, wouldn't this be easier for them both if she was in the same town? There was a third reason he was doing this, too. No child of his would ever feel abandoned. Not ever.

"I'll call Curtis tomorrow. I'm not going to lose another chance to be a father."

On Friday morning, Corrie's dad was up and scrambling eggs before she was even dressed. She poured two cups of decaf coffee and yawned. She hadn't gotten much sleep last night. Every encounter with Sam showed her a little more vividly how deep her feelings went for him. Last night she'd wanted him to tell her she meant something to him and that's why he didn't want her to move away. Maybe when they discussed this…

Her father divided the scrambled eggs in half and pushed them onto two plates. "You didn't want to talk about Sam Barclay last night. Are you ready to talk about him this morning?"

She and her dad had trod on difficult territory this week and she did feel a little closer to him. "What do you want to know?"

"What kind of man he is. You chose him to father your child for a reason. What was it?" He handed her her plate of scrambled eggs.

Corrie gave her dad his mug of coffee. "Sam's partner was the one who first interviewed me when I came to Rapid Creek. He was all business, saw me as an employee and that was fine with me. But when I met Sam—" She'd skip over the tingles she felt up her spine. "He treated me as an equal. We had the same philosophy about pets and their care and within a week I knew he was different from Eric. He didn't look over me, he looked at me. When we had a conversation and I was talking, he didn't cut in because what he had to say was more important. There was a respect about Sam—for people, for animals, just for life in general. As his sister-in-law says, he's one of the good guys." She set her plate of scrambled eggs on the counter, added milk and sugar to her coffee, then took a sip.

"He likes you."

"We work together."

"No, Corrie. I mean, he likes you in the way a man likes a woman."

She felt her cheeks start to flush and hope fill her heart. "Dad—"

"It's your business, but he seemed a little put out when I told him you were considering moving back to Minneapolis."

Was she seriously considering it? Her father had made the suggestion and she'd seen it as an option. But she *couldn't* leave Sam. Knowing the way he already felt about their baby, she wouldn't move that far away. She loved him. Yet she couldn't tell him. She didn't want him to feel sorry for her. If she took the job as director of the shelter she'd have a busy enough life to distract her from thinking about Sam. She'd have a baby and work, and maybe someday her feelings for him would simply be friendship.

On the other hand, if they grew closer because of the baby, maybe…just maybe…more would develop. She'd protected herself against that. She'd told herself if she didn't make love with him again she could stop loving him. Yet she knew now she couldn't protect herself from love. Last night as she'd lain in bed, she'd thought about what Sara had said about loyalty. Sam was a loyal man. If he promised he'd be faithful, maybe…just maybe…he'd keep that promise.

All of it was a moot point if he didn't have feelings for her. Desire wasn't the same thing as love. "Sam wants to be near his baby. He wants to see his child growing up. I can see him rocking our baby, giving him a piggyback ride, going to the school's open houses and being so proud of his little girl's or his little boy's artwork. Sam will put everything into being a dad. I can't keep his child from him."

"If you stay here, *I* won't see you very often," her dad grumbled. "We've made progress this week, haven't we? I mean, I don't think you hate me as much as you used to."

"I don't hate you. I thought I did. I wanted to. After you and Mom divorced, I couldn't see you because I *did* love you. I loved Mom. She was the one who was hurt. She was the one who needed me."

"I know what I did to us, Corrie. When I got sick a couple of months ago, I tried to look at it all honestly, not what I wanted to remember but what actually happened. Your mom and I should have gotten counseling. But my pride—" he shook his head "—my pride stood in the way of that. It stood in the way of me convincing her to forgive me after my second marriage didn't work out. It kept me from really connecting with you all these years."

"I didn't let you connect," she admitted.

"I could have pushed harder. I *should* have pushed harder. Especially after your mother died." He rubbed his hand up and down his neck. "I made so many mistakes, most of all because of pride. If you let pride stand in the way of love, you'll never be happy. *I* was never happy."

Corrie could see the emotion in her dad's eyes, hear the catch in his voice. Holding on to anger and resentment weren't good for her, either. "My son or daughter's going to need a granddad. I'll drive down to see you and you can drive up. And maybe there's something else you should think about. When are you going to retire?"

"In a year or so. I'm going to sell my business and that should give me a nice nest egg."

"Would you think about moving to Rapid Creek? Your nest egg might stretch further up here."

He laughed. "You and a baby would be enough reason to move up here. You'd really want me to do that?"

"If you think you could be happy here. I've felt so alone for the past few years." The lump in her throat swelled and she couldn't seem to get any more words out.

Seeing her predicament, her dad came to her and awkwardly put his arm around her. "You're not alone. It's time we joined forces instead of letting pride and hurt stand in our way. Don't you think?"

"I agree," she said. And then she gave her dad a real hug. The kind she hadn't given him since she was twelve.

Chapter Thirteen

Corrie loved Sam. She was going to take a giant risk and tell him.

She closed the door to the kennel, took a deep breath and wiped her damp palms on her smock. Sam had asked her to meet him in his office when she'd finished bedding down the animals for the night. She knew what he wanted to talk about—joint custody. She was ready now, not only to talk about their baby but about *them*.

When her dad had left on Sunday, she'd thought about everything they'd talked about, most of all how pride could get in the way of love. She'd let pride and fear keep her isolated for much too long. She was going to open her heart to Sam and hope that he had feelings for her, too. Yes, it was a monumental risk, but one she was willing to take. She was scared out of her wits, but that wouldn't keep her from doing it.

Yesterday she hadn't had time to talk to Sam about anything. It had seemed one emergency had led right into the other. They'd gone home late last night, exhausted. Today he'd had surgery all morning. This afternoon appointments were booked tight. Yet she was glad he wanted to talk now. Maybe tonight they could wind down together. Maybe tonight they could sleep in each others' arms.

The idea that Sam would be holding her all night put a smile on her face as she pushed open the door to his office and went inside. Patches greeted her. She took a moment, playfully ruffling his ears and stroking down his back a few times, trying to calm her racing heart. The dog wagged his tail enthusiastically, trotted over to Sam's desk chair and flopped down beside it.

Sam rose from his chair but stayed behind his desk. He looked so very serious. The distance between her and the desk suddenly seemed much greater than the width of the room. For the first time, she noticed that he was holding papers in his hand.

She suddenly felt as if she had lockjaw. Making her lips move, she asked, "What did you want to see me about?"

The expression on his face told her this wasn't about spending the night together, kissing again or even her taking the job at the animal shelter.

His dark-brown eyes were filled with turmoil as he handed her the papers. "I'd like you to read these and sign them. I think the terms are fair."

Fair? She had the feeling *fair* wasn't a word she was going to use when she was finished reading those papers.

After she digested the first line, she knew this was an official document. "Did you have Sara draw this up?" She and Sara had become friends. At least she thought they had. Would Sara do this without giving her a warning?

"No. A firm in Minneapolis advised me."

Advised him. As if the two of them couldn't talk about custody without needing a mediator.

She didn't read every word. She couldn't. Her eyes were blurry. But she got the drift of the document very fast. Particular lines jumped out at her.

Joint custody.

Scheduled visitation.

Financial arrangements with cost of living increases. And even *considerations for college.*

Her stomach sank to her toes. She felt lightheaded and by the time she turned to the third page, she couldn't see a thing except the scribbles of Sam's signature. A huge sob like a giant wave was building inside of her, and she couldn't seem to get enough air. The silence in the room competed with the ringing in her ears.

Somehow, she pushed the sob down and pulled out the most important question. "Why do you think this is necessary?"

"You said you're considering moving to Minneapolis. I have to safeguard my rights. Even if you don't go to Minneapolis, if you take the job with the shelter, I want to make sure I'm more than a father on call. I want to be a real dad."

He had to safeguard his rights because he didn't trust her. He didn't trust her to be fair, so he thought a written agreement would force her to be. How stupid she had been to think he had feelings for her. How very naive of her to start believing in love again.

The old Corrie would never have shown Sam how

much he had hurt her. The old Corrie would take the agreement, find a lawyer of her own and make sure the terms were fair. But she was a different Corrie now, a Corrie who had opened herself up to friendship and desire, letting herself feel again, in spite of the risks. She was not going to leave this office until Sam knew exactly how she felt and her pride be damned!

Heartbroken tears welled in her eyes and she didn't fight them. "Don't you know I *want* you in this baby's life? Over the weekend I thought about moving to Minneapolis but I knew I couldn't. I want you to be a dad in *every* sense of the word. I don't want to be three hours away from you because you need to see our baby's first smile, his first step, his first everything. When we made love, I thought you understood I was putting my trust in you. Do you think I made love with you without being *in* love with you?"

Sam looked absolutely shocked by her words, and that hurt most of all. If he was so shocked, then he hadn't felt any of the same things. If he was so shocked, then sex had just been sex, a recreational activity, a way to fulfill a need when no other woman was around.

She'd risked her pride, all right, and now she felt like a total fool.

Grabbing a pen from the desk, she quickly signed her name on the third sheet then tossed the papers at him. "I thought our child would be raised around two people who love and trust each other. But that was just a dream I started weaving. You've just proven to me that you don't trust me and you might never be able to trust me. That's a shame, Sam, because I was prepared to put all my trust in you."

Before she said even more that would make her look

like a misguided romantic, a woman who couldn't face the reality of male and female relationships the way they existed in the world now, she fled his office.

When he didn't come after her, she knew her dreams were as intangible as stardust, and they would never come true.

Sam felt sick, absolutely sick. And he knew no doctor could cure him.

Eric elbowed him in the ribs. "Come on, partner, cheer up. Why did you come to Happy Hour if you're going to scowl at the bartender and me and everyone else you see?"

He didn't know why he'd come to the Tavern. He really didn't. When Corrie had left the clinic he'd felt...frozen, as if he couldn't move. And then when he did move, he wasn't sure where to go. He'd taken Patches upstairs to his apartment and had driven around town for a while, seriously thinking about driving north to the cabin again. But then he saw that for what it was—the urge to escape. That's what he'd done before Thanksgiving. He'd escaped.

The time in the woods had done him good. He'd found peace again. Until Corrie had disrupted that peace.

So tonight, instead of driving north, he'd driven to the Tavern, trying to find ease in the loud music, cheese fries and Scotch. His partner had already been there, flirting with one of the waitresses.

Sam looked around the place—the exposed beams, the rustic wooden tables and chairs, the fishing gear on the walls, the customers who all looked as if they were having a good time. On Tuesday night, drinks were half price and snacks were on the house. He spotted tellers from the bank, his car insurance agent, the clerk from the mini-mart who must have just gotten off duty. Way over in the corner by the jukebox, he'd spotted Alicia. He'd waited for sadness or disappointment to zing him, but neither did. Alicia was his past and he really didn't care what she did or who she danced with.

Corrie, on the other hand— Lifting his shot glass he downed his drink.

"Since when do you drink liquor straight?" Eric asked him.

"Since I screwed up my life," Sam muttered, replaying his scene with Corrie, seeing again the hurt on her face, the tears in her eyes, the soul-deep disappointment she couldn't hide.

"What do you mean you screwed up your life? What happened?"

Sam was beginning to understand, little by little, exactly what had happened. After Alicia had told him about her abortion, he'd turned off all of his emotions. He'd closed down his heart. When Corrie had asked him to be a sperm donor, a small spark had flickered again. He hadn't even known why at first. Now he did. It wasn't only the idea of having a baby that had given him a renewed outlook, it was Corrie herself.

The nights he'd made love to her he'd assured himself they were both satisfying a physical need. He was living in the moment, grabbing pleasure where he could, giving it to Corrie. But deep down, underneath that pleasure, there had been a hell of a lot more.

He'd used what had happened with Alicia as a barrier to keep Corrie at a nice safe distance. But now?

I thought our child would be raised around two people who love and trust each other.

She had been willing to trust him. She had been willing to do more than trust him.

Do you think I made love with you without being in love with you?

She was going to stay in Rapid Creek. She'd said she had begun dreaming again. Of happily ever after? With him? Had he been so dense he couldn't see what was happening to her as well as to him?

Because now he knew what those custody papers were all about. Oh, sure, they were about rights to a baby. But they were more about keeping Corrie in his life. They were more about having ties to her that couldn't be broken. He'd thought a legal agreement could do that? It wouldn't. Only *he* could do that.

He didn't want to be with Corrie because of the baby. He liked being around her. He liked talking to her. He more than liked holding her. And kissing her. And making love to her. She fired him up in a way no woman ever had. He loved her—deep-down, genuine, until-death-do-us-part love.

He swore, his throat burning from the Scotch, the country tune on the jukebox twanging in his ears.

He slid off the barstool and zipped up his jacket.

"Where are you going?" Eric asked.

"Where I should have gone in the first place. Wish me luck, because I'm going to need a boatload of it."

"Luck for what?"

"I'm going to propose to Corrie."

Sam ignored Eric's startled expression and headed for the door. He'd have the drive to Corrie's to think of everything right to say…to come up with the perfect words to ask her to forgive him.

* * *

Corrie set a cup of tea in front of Sara. Jasper had settled under the table beside her friend's foot.

"I shouldn't have called you. You didn't have to drive in here." Corrie had been devastated when she'd arrived home, and she'd picked up the phone and called Sara on impulse to tell her what had happened.

"You sounded miserable. If I can help in any way—"

"No one can help. I never should have been so stupid as to start all of this. What was I thinking?"

"You already had feelings for Sam before you asked him, didn't you?"

Corrie squeezed lemon into her tea and sat across from Sara. "Yes, I did."

"So I imagine you were thinking you'd become closer if you became pregnant."

"I thought we *had* become closer. I thought I meant more to him than a night of…of fun and games." She took a sip of her tea and carefully set her cup back on the saucer. "In a way this is all my fault. I never should have let him believe I was serious about moving to Minneapolis."

"Why did you?"

"I was still trying to hide from my feelings. I was afraid to trust him. I thought if I moved away that might be sort of what he wanted. You know, no strings. I wanted to find out for sure. But I underestimated how much he wants to be an every-day father. I think I was also hoping he'd protest because he'd miss *me*."

Sara bent to Jasper and slid a hand over his fur. "You should never have signed those papers without having a lawyer look at them."

"You're the only lawyer in town now, and I couldn't ask you."

"Because I'm Sam's sister-in-law? Since he didn't come to me, my guess is he got a name from Ben of a specialist in custody law in Minneapolis. I'd certainly be glad to look over the papers for you. And I have a friend I can call if we both have any questions."

"I left the papers with Sam. I was so upset I just had to get out of there."

"I understand. Before Nathan and I really opened our hearts to each other, I left in the middle of the night without talking to him. After I said goodbye to Kyle, I just wanted to be somewhere Nathan wasn't so I wouldn't hurt so much."

Corrie's doorbell rang and her gaze met Sara's.

"Corrie?" Sam called through the door. "Corrie, answer the door. I need to talk to you."

"Do you want me to get it?" Sara asked.

All Corrie could do was nod. She wasn't ready to face Sam yet. She wasn't. He wanted to talk about their baby and custody. She was wrestling with the problem of how to stop loving him.

When Sara answered the door, Jasper ran to Sam as he always did.

"I didn't expect to see *you* here," he said gruffly to Sara as he gave Jasper an absent pat.

Sara didn't reply, but rather just picked up her coat and purse.

Knowing she probably still looked pale and red-eyed, Corrie came into the living room. She gave Sara a hug. "Thanks."

"Don't hesitate to call me if you need anything," her friend offered as Corrie released her.

Sara squeezed Sam's arm and met his gaze. Then she closed the door behind her.

Suspecting Sam was here because he'd brought her a copy of the custody papers, Corrie attempted to turn off all the feelings she'd ever had for him. Her pride was all she had left and she used it now to keep her from looking foolish. "You were right to want everything spelled out in black and white. We should have done it from the beginning. Sara's going to look over the agreement for me, if you have my copy."

After a long look at her, Sam pulled a wad of paper out of his jacket pocket. He straightened out the papers the best he could and then he took them by the top and ripped them into strips.

"What are you doing?"

"I never should have had the papers drawn up. I should have trusted you. I should have trusted you to let me be a dad no matter what job you took or where you lived. I'm sorry, Corrie, that I didn't."

She couldn't speak. Her emotions were keeping words from finding their way into the air.

"I have so much to say to you that I don't know where to start. I want to say it all right, and if I say it wrong I'm afraid I'm going to lose you."

"Lose me?" She couldn't put the bits and pieces together—the expression on Sam's face, the torn strips of paper that were littering the floor, the near desperation in his voice.

"I'd never keep your baby from you, Sam." Her words wobbled and it was the most she could speak. After all, that's what he was concerned about, wasn't it? His baby?

He took her by the shoulders then. "This isn't about

the baby anymore, or about me being the sperm donor. It's about you and me. Before you came to the cabin, I thought I was moving on, getting my life back together again. Your plan seemed the perfect way to do it. But then—but then I wanted to be with you more. I wanted to kiss you again. I wanted to make love to you. I didn't call it that in my head. I called it attraction. I called it chemistry. I called it everything but what it was. Love. I've fallen in love with you, Corrie. I love you."

"Sam, if you're saying this because of the baby, because you want to make sure—"

"If you weren't pregnant I would still be saying what I'm saying. I didn't even want to consider the possibility of love because I thought I couldn't trust another woman. That's what those papers were about, a remnant of what I left behind. But when I looked in your eyes earlier, when I saw your hurt and I knew I had done that, I understood you're not selfish like my mother…like Alicia. You're a giving, loving woman who needs someone to give to you. I want to be that someone. I want to be committed to you for the rest of our lives. I want a future with you."

"Oh, Sam."

He wrapped her into his arms close to his chest. His kiss was hot and possessive and all-consuming. Corrie didn't hesitate to give him what he asked for—her desire, her trust, her love.

He broke the kiss but only to take her face into his hands, to look into her eyes, to smile and ask, "Will you marry me?"

For years Corrie had told herself she'd never get married. She'd never be able to trust a man. She'd never believe he could be faithful. But this was Sam. He understood what family was all about. He was loyal and honest, and he knew how to love. She could feel his love now. She could see it in his eyes. And she wanted it, and him, in her life forever. "Yes, I'll marry you."

Sam laughed, swung her off the floor and laughed some more, as Jasper barked his excitement and approval.

Then he kissed her again, swung her up into his arms and carried her to her bedroom. "We're going to remember tonight even after we've been married fifty years," he promised.

She believed him.

Epilogue

Corrie drove Sam's van down a secondary road toward the site of their new house.

"I'm so glad Ben could fly in this weekend to help the guys lay the floors," Sara said from the passenger seat. "When Galen insisted on helping, too, I know Sam was worried. But I think giving him the job of overseer will make everything run more smoothly. He can help where he's needed but not exert himself too much. They're going to be grateful for the lemonade and iced tea we have in the jugs. I think they picked the hottest weekend in August to do this."

"Our house will be even more special knowing they all worked on it together," Corrie assured her sister-in-law who became more like a real sister every day.

Corrie was almost six months pregnant now. Since Sara couldn't have children, Corrie hadn't known how her sister-in-law would feel about being around her. But Sara was excited about Corrie's pregnancy, helped her shop for the baby and always had time to talk about what mattered to them both as newlyweds and mothers. Sara had confided that she and Nathan had applied to adopt.

"How soon do you think you'll be able to move in?" Sara asked.

"A few weeks. Most of my things are in storage since I've been living with Sam. The dogs will be thrilled when they have a yard to run in."

"When will the shelter officially open?"

"We're aiming for October first."

"How's Sam's new vet assistant working out?"

"Just great. With her kids off to college now, and three cats and two dogs of her own, she's capable and efficient. I would have snatched her up for the shelter, but Sam interviewed her first.

"Potholes ahead," Corrie announced, as she turned onto the dirt road that led to the house. She and Sara both braced themselves as she carefully drove the van down the rutted lane that was to be paved next week.

The two-story house was simple in design. The wide front porch and the brick facing kept it from being ordinary.

Before Corrie and Sara could climb out of the van, Sam and Nathan came out the front door and galloped down the porch steps, Jasper and Patches at their heels. The men were shirtless. Both wore jeans and running shoes. Nathan went to Sara and gave her a long kiss. Sam took Corrie into his arms and did the same. She loved the scent of him, the heat of him, the total man that was Sam. She'd never been happier than she had since the night Sam proposed. He made her feel desired and loved and so safe. Whenever they were together they had so much to talk about…when they weren't making love.

When Sam broke away he informed them, "The living room floor is finished and we're starting on the bedrooms. We should be able to nail on the baseboards before Ben flies home tomorrow. His experience with Habitat for Humanity when he was in college paid off."

Sara motioned to the back of the van. "We brought lunch, along with lots of lemonade and iced tea." She moved to the side door to open it.

"Don't think *you're* going to carry any of it." Sam waved to the front door of the house. "Go look at the floor."

Corrie exchanged a knowing glance with Sara. Both of their husbands were protective.

Once inside, they found Galen and Ben putting finishing touches on the living room. With its native-rock fireplace and dark-oak floor it was impressive.

Seeing them, both men came over and gave them hugs. Ben's T-shirt molded to the muscles of his arms and his flat stomach. Corrie didn't know Ben very well. When he'd flown in for their wedding in April, he'd seemed a bit aloof. But this trip he'd brought a teddy bear for the baby, and he'd had a couple of long conversations with her, as if he'd wanted to get to know her.

A half hour later they were all finishing sandwiches and sipping lemonade. Lawn chairs had been provided for Sara and Corrie, while the guys sat on the fireplace hearth, Jasper and Patches sleeping close by.

Sam fed Corrie a strawberry, gave her a passionate kiss, then said, "I'll be right back." He and Nathan left together.

Beside her, Ben confided, "I think he missed you this

morning. He couldn't stop talking about you. He's proud of the work you're doing with the shelter."

"We're newlyweds," she joked. "But I'm hoping we can feel like this for the next fifty years."

A beeping noise sounded and Corrie realized it was Ben's cell phone.

He dug it out of his pocket, opened it and checked the number, then stuffed it back again.

"Not important?" she asked.

"I can take care of it later. I don't want to spoil the moment."

"It's work?"

"It's always work." He gave her a smile, but this one wasn't a real smile.

"Sam says you need to get away from it more often."

"I rarely get a night off, let alone a weekend away."

Corrie cocked her head and studied him. "So you decided just to drop everything to help Sam lay a floor?"

Ben clasped his hands between his knees, looked down at them and then glanced back at her. "My boss suggested I get out of town for a couple of days so that's what I did."

There was definitely something he wasn't telling her. Or any of them. "Because you needed a break?"

"Just because," Ben said blandly. "Hey, look. I think Sam has a present for you."

Sam was carrying in a caned wooden rocker with a big blue bow. Nathan carried another one in behind him. The back on one rocker was a little lower than the back on the other.

Sam set the rocker beside Corrie and then knelt in front of her. "I wanted to buy something special for our new house."

Corrie looked down at her engagement ring and wedding band. They fitted together intricately. Her diamond was a heart shape because Sam had wanted to give her something special with that, too.

"His and hers rockers?" she guessed.

"They're supposed to last a lifetime, even if we put them on the porch. We can use them to rock the baby. Do you like them?"

She wrapped her arms around his neck. "I love them. And I love you."

Every time she said the words she got teary-eyed, and Sam knew that. In spite of the fact his whole family was watching, he kissed her, renewing their vows and renewing their commitment to love each other for a lifetime.

* * * * *

*Coming in September 2008—the third book in Karen Rose Smith's DADS IN PROGRESS miniseries for Silhouette Special Edition.
In THE DADDY VERDICT, assistant district attorney Ben Barclay (Sam and Nathan's brother) discovers that a marriage of convenience leads to true love.*